MW00619856

ADVANCE PRAISE FOR *SMALL MARVELS*

"Scott Russell Sanders, being a wise man who agonizes over the sinking of our traditional virtues, uses his great storytelling skills to keep buoying them up. In *Small Marvels*, he reminds us of the values of honest work, unselfishness, and wholesome family devotion, not by preaching but by pulling us into warm, funny, whimsical stories about the poor but happy family of Gordon Mills, a homely jack-of-all-trades who can leave no good deed undone. Gordon is the worthiest poor-folks' hero I've seen since Wendell Berry's unforgettable *Jayber Crow*." —James Alexander Thom, author of *Fire in the Water*

"Scott Russell Sanders has created a literature encompassing the natural world, our sense of place, and the ways in which we can build community that lasts. This collection of linked stories about an unwieldy, yet loving family in what might, at first glance, seem like the middle of nowhere is a tender addition to a generous body of work." —David Hoppe, author of *Midcentury Boy*

"This book is a marvel indeed—a charming, improbably generous portrait of the pleasures of small-town life and enduring values. Simultaneously funny, rueful, nostalgic, and wry, these stories embrace hope and endurance, finding the miraculous bound up in the mundane. As one character says, 'Earth was home to more marvels than he could take in.'" —Erin McGraw, author of *Joy and 52 Other Very Short Stories*

"Scott Russell Sanders's newest book, *Small Marvels*, makes me feel better about the world. Each story from the lives of Gordon Mills and his family is a gift and the collection as a whole is a balm for the heart and spirit. In a time of uncertainty and division, Gordon (who is part mechanic, part everyday mystic) and his very human, always entertaining family, reminds us of all that is still right in the world and shines a light on what is luminous and extraordinary in an ordinary day. Scott Russell Sanders has a beautiful constellation of works, I have loved all I've encountered, and *Small Marvels* is truly another bright star." —Carrie Newcomer, songwriter, author of *Until Now, The Beautiful Not Yet, Until Now: New Poems*

"Like the stories of Jim Heynen or Wendell Berry, the missives found in Scott Russell Sanders's *Small Marvels* are finely finished finishes of bulletins and billet-doux that lap and layer 'place' into Place, creating a depth by means of gritty sanding and steel-wooled buffing on what was once the flat and dull surface of the world's old spoil. America's drama has always been between mobility and stability. These deadpan understated dispatches from the striations of Limestone are all about the staunch staying, and these tales sculpt, indeed, poetic stays against the entropic confusion found in all our hyperkinetic need for the getting up and the going."

—Michael Martone, author of *The Complete Writings of Art Smith, The Bird Boy of Fort Wayne, Edited by Michael Martone* and *The Moon Over Wapakoneta*

"Scott Russell Sanders's *Small Miracles* is its own kind of miracle, a contemporary work of short fiction where the protagonist, Gordon Mills, quietly repairs the work of entropy with love and kindness, a ready set of a handyman's tools, and an unshakable faith in community. I love this character, his family, and the town of Limestone, Indiana, a place reminiscent of Wendell Berry's Port William, that they call home."

—Susan Neville, author of *The Town of Whispering Dolls*

"There is nothing small about this epic, large-hearted, greatly imagined book. Of all of his serious books on the fate of our earth, this may be Sanders's most honest of all, a brave look at the realities of a struggling life in a literal holy landscape. We need this poignant, deeply comical book to remind us what a good time we can have after all in this world, right at home, with each other, in the most basic and fantastic of ways."

—Barbara Mossberg, author of *Here for the Present*

ALSO BY SCOTT RUSSELL SANDERS

NONFICTION

Stone Country
The Paradise of Bombs
Secrets of the Universe
Staying Put: Making a Home in a Restless World
Writing from the Center
Hunting for Hope: A Father's Journeys
The Country of Language
The Force of Spirit
A Private History of Awe
A Conservationist Manifesto
Earth Works: Selected Essays
Stone Country: Then and Now
The Way of Imagination

FICTION

Wilderness Plots
Fetching the Dead
Wonders Hidden: Audubon's Early Years
Hear the Wind Blow: American Folksongs Retold
Terrarium
Bad Man Ballad
The Engineer of Beasts
The Invisible Company
Divine Animal
Dancing in Dreamtime

*small
marvels*

small marvels

stories

SCOTT RUSSELL SANDERS

Indiana University Press

This book is a publication of

Indiana University Press
Office of Scholarly Publishing
Herman B Wells Library 350
1320 East 10th Street
Bloomington, Indiana 47405 USA

iupress.org

© 2022 by Scott Russell Sanders

All rights reserved
No part of this book may be reproduced
or utilized in any form or by any means,
electronic or mechanical, including
photocopying and recording, or by any
information storage and retrieval system,
without permission in writing from the
publisher. The paper used in this publication
meets the minimum requirements of the
American National Standard for Information
Sciences—Permanence of Paper for Printed
Library Materials, ANSI Z39.48-1992.

Manufactured in the
United States of America

First Printing 2022

The author and publisher gratefully
acknowledge the following publications,
in which earlier versions of stories from
this book first appeared: *Arts Indiana*
("Dance"); *Beloit Fiction Journal* ("Fossil");
Bloom Magazine ("Crows," "Rabbit," and
"Aurora," originally titled "Southern Lights");
Gettysburg Review ("Smoke," "Weight," and
"Maintenance," originally titled "Night
Calls"); *Hawk & Handsaw* ("Flood"); *Hopewell
Review* ("Snow," originally titled "July Snow");
Bryan Furuness, ed., *An Indiana Christmas*
("Wealth"); *Potlatch* ("Wilderness," originally
titled "The Wilds"); *Village Advocate*
("Trash"); and William Shore, ed., *Voices
Louder Than Words* ("Worry," originally titled
"Harm's Reach"). The author also gratefully
acknowledges that the story "Rabbit" was
inspired by Carrie Newcomer's song "Forever
Ray," which appears in her album *A Permeable
Life* (Available Light Records, 2014).

Library of Congress Cataloging-in-
 Publication Data

Names: Sanders, Scott R. (Scott Russell),
 author.
Title: Small marvels : stories / Scott Russell
 Sanders.
Description: Bloomington, Indiana : Indiana
 University Press, [2022]
Identifiers: LCCN 2021053241 (print) | LCCN
 2021053242 (ebook) | ISBN 9780253061980
 (hardback) | ISBN 9780253061997
 (paperback) | ISBN 9780253062000 (ebook)
Subjects: LCSH: Indiana—Fiction. | LCGFT:
 Short stories.
Classification: LCC PS3569.A5137 S63 2022
 (print) | LCC PS3569.A5137 (ebook) | DDC
 813/.54—dc23/eng/20211116
LC record available at https://lccn.loc
 .gov/2021053241
LC ebook record available at https://lccn.loc
 .gov/2021053242

For the Wilderness Plots *troupe, with gratitude and affection—*
Krista Detor
Tim Grimm
Jan Lucas
Robert Meitus
Carrie Newcomer
Tom Roznowski
Dave Weber
Michael White

"Love all God's creation, the whole and every grain of sand in it. Love every leaf, every ray of God's light. Love the animals, love the plants, love everything. If you love everything, you will perceive the divine mystery in things."

—FATHER ZOSIMA in Fyodor Dostoevsky's
The Brothers Karamazov

CONTENTS

1 *Aurora*

5 *Trees*

12 *Sisters*

19 *Parents*

27 *Widows*

35 *Smoke*

44 *Centaur*

49 *Blues*

55 *Wealth*

61 *Maintenance*

68 *Weight*

77 *Dance*

83 *Crows*

87 *Rabbit*

91 *Fossil*

103 *Trash*

112 *Alligators*

119 *Worry*

130 *Wolf*

141 *Wilderness*

151 *Snow*

CONTENTS

157 *Dinosaur*

166 *Anniversary*

181 *Flood*

small marvels

Aurora

Once, not long ago, there was a jack-of-all-trades named Gordon Mills who lived with his wife, their four children, and three grandparents in Limestone, Indiana, a city tucked away among forested hills and shadowy caves, a place so obscure that it rarely appears on maps. Their old house, which fell apart as fast as Gordon could fix it, was packed with souls from foundation to rafters. Gordon slept in the basement with his wife, a small but formidable woman named Mabel. They had surrendered their former bedroom to Mabel's parents, who were a bit doddery, while his mother, still spry, slept in a room Gordon had built over the garage. The two daughters, prone to squabbling, occupied separate bedrooms on the second floor, while the two sons, far enough apart in age to avoid fighting, shared bunk beds in the attic.

They weren't exactly poor, since they never went hungry, but they also never had any spare cash to put away for harder times. Each month Mabel's parents, Mamaw and Papaw Hawkins, received a tiny social security check, which they used to order surefire remedies for old age from ads in the back pages of magazines. Gordon's mother, Granny Mills, drew an even tinier pension from the owners of the quarry in which his father had been crushed by a tumbled limestone block. She spent much of her money on lottery tickets and trips to the French Lick Casino, without much luck. The older children worked odd jobs after school, but the few dollars they brought in went for clothes, music, books, and electronic gadgets. Mabel had her hands full running the household. That left Gordon to earn enough to keep food on the table and a roof over their heads.

Still, they managed to scrape by on Gordon's wages from the city maintenance crew and the extra bucks he pulled in from doing odd jobs on weekends. Blessed with the constitution of an ox, he never called in sick and never turned down overtime. He could do pretty much anything that needed doing, so long as it didn't involve using a phone or a computer. He could repair sidewalks, pave streets, cut up fallen trees, weld a broken chassis, wire a stoplight, and run every sort of machine. One week he might be tuning up snowplows for winter, and the next he might be digging up a broken sewer main, and the next he might be scrubbing graffiti from the water tower or replacing the roof on a bus shelter after a tornado. Whenever a job cropped up that nobody else could do, Gordon got the call, which is how he came to be known in local lore as the man who coaxed the crows from their roosts on the courthouse square and chased alligators out of the sewage lagoon and cleaned up after the rare beasts that took up residence in one of the local caves.

Gordon had begun learning his many trades as an infant, when he played with wrenches, pliers, and hammers instead of stuffed animals. The tools weren't wooden toys either, but real ones, placed in the crib by Gordon's father, who earned a living with his hands and figured he'd better prepare his son to do the same. Gordon's mother, uncertain how to treat the baby's diaper rash, followed her husband's advice by using lithium grease, which worked like a charm, although it made Gordon smell like an engine. He was her first child and also, as it turned out, her last. She and her husband kept trying for another one, year after year, right up until the quarry accident put an end to their efforts, but they had no more luck in bed than she would have later on at the casino.

It was as though Gordon, one of the burliest babies ever delivered in the Limestone hospital, had used up all the time on her biological clock.

When his father died, Gordon quit school, lied about his age, joined the navy, and spent his seven-year hitch in the Seabees, building airstrips, barracks, and bunkers in the Persian Gulf, all the while sending paychecks to his mother. Then he returned home, his body intact but wounded in the depths of his heart, where he rarely probed. When he applied for a job with the city maintenance crew, the supervisor sized him up with raised eyebrows, then challenged him to figure out what was wrong with a balky garbage truck that had baffled the mechanics. Gordon soon had it purring, and the supervisor hired him on the spot.

It so happened that Gordon's first job for the city was driving that garbage truck up and down the streets of Limestone before dawn in the dead of winter, while two teenage boys, recently expelled from high school, rode on the rear bumper and emptied trashcans into the hopper. Once the truck was loaded, Gordon dropped the boys at the service garage to warm up while he drove out to the landfill. He remembered the place from before it became the municipal dump, when it was a valley where he hunted for mushrooms in the shade of beeches in spring, ate pawpaws and blackberries in summer, gathered walnuts and hickory nuts in the fall, and tracked deer with his father in winter. Now the valley was buried under a heap of rubbish that rose higher than the surrounding hills.

When he reached the top of the garbage mound that first morning on the job, he noticed along the northern horizon a glow the bluish color of the flame on a gas stove. It was the wrong direction for sunrise. Besides, the rest of the sky was still as black as the inside of a cat. He stopped, tilted the hopper, and then pumped the brake a few times as he eased forward, jostling the truck until it was empty. Meanwhile, the glow on the horizon turned violet and began to ripple like a windblown curtain. He watched until the rising sun buttered the sky.

The next morning he persuaded one of the loaders to ride with him on the first run to the dump, and sure enough, there was the shimmery

3

glow, this time the color of copper. But the boy saw nothing, merely shrugged before dozing off. The following day the second boy rode along, but he also failed to see the shimmer.

On the third morning, the maintenance supervisor agreed to go, grousing the whole way, and even though he squinted, he couldn't make out the rippling greenish veils. "You sure you're not hitting the bottle, Mills?" he asked.

"I never drink," said Gordon. "Booze killed my dad."

"I thought he died in a quarry accident."

"He did, but only because he got drunk at lunch and fell asleep right where the derrick set down a ten-ton stone."

The supervisor winced. "Well, then if you're not sloshed, you'd better get your eyes checked. Besides, if fancy lights really do start waving around in the sky, you think they'd shine down on a dump?"

Gordon had no theory about what might or might not shine down on a dump or about anything else the world might serve up when he happened to be looking. He just kept his eyes peeled. During the rest of that winter, he often spied the northern glow from atop the mountain of trash but never from anywhere else. The landfill crew only scoffed when he asked if they had noticed the blaze flickering at the edge of the world. So he told nobody else about his discovery until years later, after settling into marriage with Mabel, when he took a ride to the dump before dawn with their long-awaited firstborn, a tot named Jeanne, who clapped her hands in wonder at the dancing lights.

Trees

To celebrate the birth of his first child, Gordon Mills planted a tree in the yard, and he did the same when his other three children were born. For Jeanne, the first, it was a sugar maple. For Bruce, who came along next, it was a red oak. For his third child, Veronica, he planted a sycamore, and for Danny, last of all, he planted a tulip tree. After Danny's birth, Mabel declared herself retired from the baby-making business, and her word was law on such matters. On most other matters as well, truth be told. Besides, with trees occupying all four corners of their one-acre lot and a vegetable garden claiming the sunniest spot, the rest of the yard was reserved for the trove of scrap lumber, defunct appliances, miscellaneous machine parts, and other potentially useful stuff that Gordon collected, a habit learned from his father.

The sugar maple soon formed a canopy shaped like an egg, rounded at the top and bottom and neatly tapering on the sides, and it turned scarlet in the fall. In sympathy with her tree, Jeanne grew up to appear tidy and composed on the outside, but her red hair suggested a fiery interior. The oak leaves turned the color of rubies for a spell in the fall, as if they had been hiding jewels all summer, but then they sobered to brown and clung to the tree all winter, clattering in the breeze. Like his oak, Bruce was sturdy and secretive, allowing flashes of brilliance to show through every once in a while with a wisecrack or an invention and then retreating behind the mop of brown hair that nearly covered his eyes.

By contrast, Veronica dramatized her moods the way her sycamore flung out its branches and flaunted its bark, a crazy quilt of light and dark patches, and her long hair was as black as a crow's wing. Like her tree, she loved water, opened her arms to every sort of animal, and gleamed in sunlight. Danny grew as straight and fast as the tulip tree, which he began climbing soon after he learned to walk and which he continued climbing in spite of having tumbled out and broken his arm, a mishap in keeping with the character of his tree, whose limbs often cracked in high winds. Like the tulip tree, he mended quickly and kept sprouting skyward, with eyes as green as any spring leaf and hair as golden as any leaf in fall.

Given these resemblances, it wasn't surprising that all four children became fierce defenders of trees. They made sure every piece of cardboard and scrap of paper in the Mills household was recycled. They joined picket lines outside local building-supply stores that bought lumber from old-growth stands. They wrote letters to the president and the governor, protesting clear-cuts in the state and national forests. With money from their allowances and later on with earnings from odd jobs, they sponsored the planting of trees in the Amazon, in Africa, and across America. They showed up at every Arbor Day celebration with shovels, eager to nestle roots into the soil.

Jeanne called herself a tree hugger in honor of those women in India who wrapped their arms around trees to prevent loggers from felling their village forests. Bruce identified with the druids, sporting a long robe and carrying a staff on ceremonial occasions and trying his best to grow a beard. Veronica fancied herself a wood sprite, which gave her the opportunity to wear flowers in her hair, frilly dresses, and gauzy wings. Danny wished he could take a break from being a kid and become a tree—not forever, just long enough to root his legs in the ground, feel squirrels scampering up his ribs, and hear birds singing in his hair.

So you can imagine how riled up the Mills children became when the mayor of Limestone announced plans to clear a grove of trees from a city park to allow for expansion of the jail. Jeanne circulated a petition against the plan at the college, where she was studying biology and art history. Bruce took the petition to the high school, Veronica to her middle school, and Danny to his elementary school.

At first the teachers thought this would be a good way of teaching civic responsibility, but the movement soon got out of hand. Before long, children were pestering school principals to sign the petition and badgering their parents to call the mayor. They filled their class-rooms with tree posters, plastered shop windows with signs proclaim-ing GROW FORESTS NOT PRISONS, and flooded the newspaper with letters. Instead of enlarging the jail, the letters argued, why not arrest fewer people? Or if a bigger jail really was needed, why not expand in the other direction and take over the sheriff's parking lot? It would do the paunchy sheriff and his equally paunchy deputies a lot of good if they had to walk a few blocks to reach their squad cars, the letters pointed out. Besides, it was a well-established fact that patients in hos-pitals healed faster if they could look out on a bit of nature, so wouldn't sight of that green park help rehabilitate prisoners? Thanks to the zeal of the kids, dinner table conversations all across the city kept circling back to the endangered grove of trees.

Meanwhile, dressed in his druid's outfit, Bruce pitched a tent in the park and made himself at home. Wearing her wood sprite getup, com-plete with wings, Veronica wove pink yarn in and out among the trees, forming a delicate web and tying a bow around each trunk. Jeanne brought a contingent of biology students to erect banners documenting the ecological benefits of forests, including charts about water filtra-tion and carbon sequestration and other matters that puzzled pass-ersby. Danny clambered high into the branches, where he conversed with birds and studied clouds. Before the police could shoo them away, dozens of other kids showed up with tarps and tents and sleeping bags. So the chief of police issued a warning and called the mayor, who was up for reelection in a couple of months.

"Better let them have their fun," the mayor advised. "They'll go running home as soon as it rains."

But the children didn't flee when it rained. Instead, night by night the encampment grew. School bus drivers adjusted their routes so they could pick up students there in the morning and drop them there in the afternoon. In the evenings, teachers held tutoring sessions under the trees. Unable to persuade their children to come home, mothers delivered meals and fresh clothes. Fathers patrolled the park boundary to keep out thugs. To protect the camp during the day while the kids were in school, Granny Mills and Mamaw and Papaw Hawkins set up lawn chairs in the park and chatted with friends who happened by, and soon there were dozens of oldsters lounging about, playing checkers or bridge on card tables, reading books, strumming guitars, and shooting the breeze. Many of them, it turned out, had loved trees in secret all along but were afraid their friends might find such love eccentric.

After some weeks of this uproar with no sign of surrender from the protesters, the mayor called the Mills household one night. Naturally, Gordon avoided the phone until he learned the call was for him.

"Mr. Mills," the mayor began, "I understand your children started all this trouble. I also understand you're a valued employee in the city maintenance department. Do you like your job?'

"I sure do," Gordon replied.

"Then I suggest you rein in your offspring—and your mother and your wife's parents, while you're at it—because I'd hate for the city to lose the services of a dedicated worker like yourself."

Gordon talked it over with Mabel in bed that night. "How can you tell them to quit?" she said. "You set them on this path when you planted those saplings. Besides, the kids are right."

"Them being right won't keep food on the table if I get fired," Gordon objected.

"If you get fired, I'll go door to door and campaign against the mayor. I'll raise such a stink it will draw vultures to circle over city hall."

Knowing Mabel would do all of that and more once she got her dander up, Gordon settled into fitful sleep.

At work the next day, the maintenance supervisor told him that word of the mayor's anger had come down from on high. "He thinks you're trying to make him look bad before the election," the supervisor said. "Since I'd have to hire three men to replace you, I'm going to help you solve this little family problem."

"How's that?" Gordon asked.

"As soon as the kids go off to school, I'm going to send you with a crew to clean up the park. There'll be a couple dozen cops on hand to roust out the old-timers. All you've got to do is tear down the camp and throw everything in the truck and haul it to the dump. Easy as pie. Then the mayor's happy, I'm happy, you're happy, and the city's at peace."

Gordon thought for a minute before saying, "I quit."

"What do you mean, quit? You can't quit."

Without answering, Gordon picked up his lunch box and headed for the door.

"Where are you going?" the supervisor yelled.

"To see my kids."

When Gordon reached the park, he found a ring of policemen surrounding the camp, where the youngsters, skipping school for the day, were huddled in their tents or talking in little clumps or sitting in the branches of trees. The sight of Danny waving from high up in a shagbark hickory tugged Gordon right through the police barricade. He ignored orders to stop, and when hands grabbed at him, he shook loose and kept going. The police backed off when he was engulfed by a mob of kids, including Bruce the druid, Veronica the wood sprite, and Jeanne the red-haired rebel. Nimble as any squirrel, Danny scurried down the hickory and leaped from the lowest branch into Gordon's arms.

While the police chief muttered into a walkie-talkie, a crowd began to gather from near and far. There were shoppers, joggers, office workers, dog walkers, elderly ramblers, bleary-eyed parents pushing baby buggies, cooks in aprons, carpenters in overalls, monks in robes, yoga enthusiasts in leotards—every sort of person under the sun. Soon television crews arrived in satellite trucks, newspaper photographers showed up with cameras clicking, reporters began scribbling notes, and political candidates turned out to shake hands and distribute campaign buttons, all of them drawn there by rumors that the mayor was going to make an important announcement in the park at nine o'clock that morning.

The rumors, it so happened, had been set in motion by Mabel, who had called her friends, who had called their friends, who had in turn called their own friends, and so on, until almost everyone in the city had heard the news except the mayor. When the mayor did hear, he decided to assert his authority by showing up at the appointed hour and declaring that the camp would be cleared and the trees would be leveled that very day. He fancied himself posing in coat and tie and holding a chain saw beside a fresh stump—a bold image for the evening news.

By the time he arrived, however, the crowd had swelled to fill the sidewalks and streets for a block in every direction from the park. He had to wade through a thicket of placards, a din of chanting, and a swirl of dancing. Only when he reached the police barricade, climbed onto a picnic table, and turned around to face the throng did he fully weigh the fact that every placard praised the trees, every chant celebrated the trees, every dance blessed the trees, and every person there age eighteen or older could vote for his opponent in the coming election.

"My fellow citizens," the mayor began, pausing to absorb these revelations and to allow time for the cameras to focus, "after careful deliberation, and with due respect for the subtleties of the case, and bearing in mind the great traditions of democracy and the sacrifices of our armed forces, and in my tireless efforts to keep your taxes low, and as an expression, I must add, of my own deep love for God's creation, I have decided"—he paused again for effect—"to spare these majestic trees—"

Whatever else he might have said was drowned out by a roar from the multitude. The mayor was staggered by the force of this joy, and he was staggered again when a small but formidable woman clambered up onto the picnic table and thumped him on the back and smacked a crown of leaves onto his head.

"You go, Mama!" Veronica cried.

For who else could it be but Mabel Mills? Beaming there beside the mayor with her gray hair billowing up like a storm cloud, she motioned to her kids, who climbed up beside her, their arms lifted like branches, prompting onlookers to think of maples and oaks, sycamores and tulip trees. The crowd cheered, and Gordon cheered loudest of all.

Sisters

As a young child, Jeanne Mills trusted animals, even worms and pill bugs and mice, for they kept no secrets. But she feared vegetables. The menace in carrots was obvious, those orange daggers. Nor was there anything subtle about the blunt clubs of cucumbers and zucchini. Peas lay hidden in their pods like bullets, and who could tell what went on among the yellow pebbles of corn hidden beneath the husk? Beets looked like bruised hearts, and potatoes might have been the lumpy toes of giants. Lettuce and cabbage were even more sinister, clutching their green hands into fists. Most frightening of all were the dense albino clouds of cauliflower and the swollen broccoli with their dark recesses.

Jeanne could read the feelings of animals in their eyes and paws and twitchy tails. But vegetables were enigmatic. They had no eyes, no mouths or tails to reveal what went on inside their slick or knobby skin. When she was still small enough to ride in the cart as Mabel shopped for groceries, Jeanne closed her eyes near the produce section, imagining the vegetables could not see her if she could not see them, and she closed her eyes again while passing the meat counter, out of sympathy for the dead chickens and pigs and cows. Naturally, she balked at anything on her plate that resembled an animal or a vegetable. She would have nothing to do with eggs once she learned where they came from. After seeing a picture of cows with rubbery pink udders drooping between their hind legs, she refused to drink milk.

Mabel wondered if these quirks were connected to the fact that Jeanne had been born two weeks late, as if reluctant to leave the womb where all nourishment came directly through the umbilical cord. The labor had lasted twelve hours, at the end of which Jeanne emerged with a mop of hair as red as her squalling face—clear signs of a stubborn temperament, according to Mabel's mother, who had given birth to three redheads of her own, including Mabel.

"When you were a toddler," Mamaw Hawkins reminded her, "you held on to your likes and dislikes as firmly as a snapping turtle on a stick."

"Was I fussy about food?" Mabel asked.

"Fussy? Every meal with you was like negotiating nuclear disarmament with the Russians. That's why you're so scrawny to this very day," added Mamaw Hawkins, who was shaped like a moon of Jupiter, and not a lesser moon either. "The only way I could get you to eat a bite was by trickery."

Coached by her mother, Mabel became an expert at disguising food. She would hide puréed lamb, turkey, spinach, or rutabaga in applesauce. She would bake bread with soy flour, stir extra eggs into pancakes, mix peanut butter into oatmeal. Jeanne inspected these offerings skeptically, but eventually succumbed to the sweetness of apples or syrup or jam. Still, a few more strands of Mabel's hair turned gray with each meal. At this rate, her skull would soon be covered like her mother's, with a helmet of permed white curls.

Mabel never dreamed that a solution to Jeanne's vegetable jitters would come from Gordon, whose appetite was prodigious. What could he know about food phobias, this man who ate with gusto anything and everything she put on his plate? Before making a trip to the grocery store, she had to check the refrigerator and pantry to find out what he had devoured when she wasn't looking. So it came as a surprise when Gordon announced over breakfast one Saturday in spring that he and Jeanne, then age six, were going to plant the garden.

"What garden?" Mabel asked, for they had never grown more than a scruffy patch of grass in their backyard, which was crowded with stacks of lumber, broken-down machines, rusting appliances, and other scavenged stuff that Gordon thought might come in handy one day.

"The garden of the three sisters," he said.

Jeanne perked up. "What sisters?" So far, she had only a little brother named Brucie, who was mainly a nuisance.

"You'll see," Gordon said. "But first you've got to clean your plate."

Jeanne did clean her plate, with less pouting than usual and no tears. Then she scampered upstairs to change into her bib overalls, a miniature version of those Gordon wore, and the two of them went outside. From the kitchen sink, Mabel watched them clear junk from the sunniest part of the backyard, Gordon lugging the heavy items and Jeanne carrying the light ones. Then he began spading up the dirt, which looked surprisingly rich, and Jeanne came behind him, crumbling the clods by stomping on them with her rubber boots. Next, Gordon raked the loosened soil into mounds laid out in three rows, and Jeanne pulled her own little rake right after him, careful not to harm the worms. Then the two of them bent over each mound, poking in seeds with their fingers and covering the holes with dirt.

When they came in for lunch, Jeanne washed up without balking, excitedly telling Mabel that the three sisters were corn, beans, and squash. "We planted them just like the Iroquois do," she explained, carefully pronouncing the new word, EAR-uh-COY, she had just learned from her daddy. "Corn in the middle to grow tall, beans in a circle around the corn to climb up the stalk, and squash in a ring around the beans to cover the ground and keep down weeds."

"Why are they called sisters?" Mabel asked.

"Because they like to live together." Jeanne gave a sly look as she asked, "Am I going to get a little sister?"

Run ragged keeping up with this six-year-old fireball and three-year-old Brucie, Mabel answered cautiously, "We'll have to see, sweetie."

During lunch, which Gordon ate with his usual zest, he waggled his bristly eyebrows at Mabel, to signal so far so good. Jeanne still pushed the food around on her plate, her enthusiasm for the three sisters not yet having overcome her fear of vegetables.

Before dawn the next morning, Jeanne tiptoed into the basement bedroom and made her way to the side of the bed where Gordon slept. She whispered into his hairy ear, "The sisters are up."

Without opening his eyes, Gordon muttered, "Not yet, kiddo. It'll take a week or two."

"Come see, Daddy," Jeanne insisted. "They're all putting up shoots!"

When he did open his eyes, Gordon could see that she was wearing her bib overalls and rubber boots and clutching a flashlight. To keep from waking Mabel, he decided to humor the impatient rascal and go outside to show her that the garden was still bare. But what they found, in the beam of the flashlight, were stalks of corn several inches tall rising from mound after mound, each sprout entwined with the tendrils of beans and surrounded by squash vines.

"Well, I'll be," Gordon said. "I guess they couldn't wait to see you."

"See me?" said Jeanne.

"Why, sure. You're the fourth sister."

Within a week, the corn had reached as high as Gordon's head, and he figured he would need a stepladder to pick the ears when they came ripe in August. In another week, Jeanne could wander among the stalks as in a forest.

All that summer, she spent every spare minute in the garden, watering the plants, pulling weeds, plucking off bean beetles and corn worms and squash bugs. Soon the pole beans began to flower—white, lavender, and pink—and bees nuzzled the blossoms. Then the corn sprouted yellow tassels that curved like the tracks of rockets on the Fourth of July, and the squash broke out in golden blossoms shaped like trumpets.

When the beans formed, they were as tiny as fingernail clippings, but they quickly grew as long and fat as the pencils Jeanne used in first grade. She was hesitant to pick them until Gordon told her they were gifts from her sisters, and then she gathered enough to fill a pot. As the beans cooked, she perched on a stool by the stove, and Mabel showed her how to tell when they were done by poking them with a fork, how to lightly salt them and dab them with butter. As soon as the beans were cool enough, Jeanne nibbled one cautiously, then another and another, each one more eagerly, until she was stuffed. Mabel had to cook up another potful to feed the rest of the family, which, back in those days, before the arrival of Veronica and Danny, included little Brucie and voracious Gordon, as well as the three grandparents.

No matter how many beans Mabel served her family, no matter how many she canned or froze, she could not keep up with the supply that Jeanne and Gordon brought in from the garden. Soon the refrigerator was chock-full, the countertops were piled high, and boxes overflowing with beans crowded the floor. Meanwhile the squash began to come ripe, some shaped like baseball bats, some like pumpkins or toads, some like blimps or flying saucers or round-bottomed gnomes. They might be green or yellow, orange or brown, speckled or striped, dark as the dirt or bright as a clown's painted face. Brucie helped Jeanne hunt for them in the jungle of giant leaves and vines that had spread over the garden, over the piles of lumber and ancient machines, over the fences into nearby yards. Each day the kids brought armfuls into the kitchen, where Mabel cooked squash every way she could imagine, from stir-fry to soup.

Even with Jeanne gobbling down these gifts from the three sisters and the rest of the Mills household eating all they could hold, Mabel soon had to send Gordon around the neighborhood pushing his wheelbarrow heaped with squash and beans to give away the excess. Jeanne set up a card table by the sidewalk and handed zucchini to passersby. The grandparents took baskets of beans to the senior center, where they unloaded their cargo by touting the life-extending virtues of vegetables. Brucie presented a round red squash each day to his preschool teacher, pretending it was an apple, and the teacher in turn shared her excess with friends. When even those outlets proved insufficient to dispose of the crop, Mabel called the Hoosier Hills Community Kitchen, which began hauling away a truckload every week or so.

Meanwhile, the corn stalks grew as high as the second-story windows, as high as the roof, as high as the chimney, as high as the sugar maple Gordon had planted in the yard when Jeanne was born. By the time the corn was ready for picking, the lower ears could be reached from a stepladder, as Gordon had predicted, but he had to build a scaffold to reach the ears higher up, and the highest ones he had to leave for the squirrels and crows. Even at the very top, where tassels shimmied in the breeze, the stalks were laced with runner beans, which kept flinging their tendrils skyward.

"Daddy," Jeanne asked, "will they climb to the land of giants?"

"To the clouds, maybe," he assured her, "but not all the way to the giants."

After they picked the first ear of corn, Gordon tugged off the husk and Jeanne rubbed away the silk. Then he invited her to take a bite.

"Without cooking?" she asked.

"Cooking is fine, but raccoons eat it just like this."

Jeanne held the tip of the ear in one hand, the stem in the other, and studied the rows of yellow pebbles, which seemed less menacing now that she had helped to grow them. Warily, she brought the corn to her mouth, nibbled a bit, and then began munching away, startled by the sweetness.

By late summer, when the corn was as its peak, the beans had petered out, and all except the butternut squash had stopped bearing. But those hardy squash were already so large, a dozen of them would fill the wheelbarrow. And the corn ripened by the bushel day after day. Every afternoon when Gordon came home from the city garage, he and Jeanne filled half a dozen grocery sacks with freshly picked ears, which they delivered to friends and strangers, leaving a bag outside each front door, ringing the bell, and dashing away. As Jeanne imagined the people in those houses discovering this gift, she wondered if they would be amazed, as she was, that the sisters had created this golden sweetness out of nothing but seeds and dirt and sun and rain.

While Mabel appreciated the bountiful harvest, she informed Gordon that she would be happier in coming years with a small fraction of that bounty, so he should reduce the size of the garden plot accordingly.

That fall, seed catalogs began arriving in the mail, as if summoned by Jeanne's change of heart, but actually summoned by Gordon, who had overcome his dread of telephones long enough to call toll-free numbers and ask for the catalogs to be sent. On winter evenings, Jeanne sat in his lap and pored over the glossy pages, marking the seeds she wished to plant in spring, and then she toddled off to bed and dreamed of vegetables.

Parents

*J*eanne grew and grew, though fortunately not as high as the corn, and soon Brucie could no longer be thought of as little and started asking to be called Bruce. These swift changes made Mabel and Gordon feel a bit blue. Then along came Veronica, a new baby to cuddle, but seemingly overnight she turned into a rambunctious toddler and soon became a gadabout who wriggled free of hugs and danced away beyond arm's reach. In compensation for those lost hugs, once Veronica started kindergarten, Mabel could rest a few minutes during the day without a child clamoring for her attention. She was just getting used to these childless spells when she discovered that another baby was on the way, and then a month or so after her fortieth birthday, along came Danny, unplanned, but the sweetest of all surprises.

Mabel's delight in this fourth child did not prevent her from making sure there would not be a fifth, beginning with firm instructions to Gordon about bedtime protocols.

"With five we could start a basketball team," he suggested.

"With five you'd have to start a new marriage," she replied.

Just how the two of them ever became husband and wife was a wonder to their children, who often rehearsed the story among themselves, but it was also an embarrassment, to be shared only with friends who could be counted on not to laugh, for like much else about their parents, it was weird. Depending on whether they told their dad's account or their mom's, the path to marriage began with either a wrestling match or a flat tire.

In telling the story, which they embroidered with their own imaginings as well as details learned from their grandparents, the children usually began with the wrestling match, since that occurred long before the flat tire.

Gordon was fifteen at the time, a sophomore in high school, a so-so student but a powerhouse wrestler. Since first laying eyes on him, the football coach had been trying to recruit him to play linebacker. But Gordon followed the path blazed by his father, Pappy Mills, who had been a champion wrestler at Limestone High School South, twice reaching the state semifinals before losing each time to the same boy, a bruiser from Fort Wayne. Who knows? If Pappy Mills had won a state title, he might have earned an athletic scholarship and gone to college. Instead, unwilling to take over the family farm, he went to work in a quarry.

While Pappy Mills had wrestled in the 189-pound class, Gordon competed at 215, which placed him among the heavyweights. Most of his opponents were guys with more flab than muscle, whereas he had more muscle than flab, partly from lifting weights but chiefly from helping out with haying, fencing, cattle feeding, and other heavy chores on his grandparents' farm. As a freshman, he beat out the senior heavyweight for the varsity spot and defeated every other heavyweight in the league, up to and including the previous champion, Sonny Hawkins, from the rival high school, Limestone North. In his sophomore year, Gordon repeated as league champion, this time defeating Butch Hawkins, the younger brother of Sonny.

The Mills children could read about these exploits in yellowed clippings from the sports pages of the *Limestone Tribune,* kept in an album by Granny Mills. She offered her own anecdotes about the young Gordon, such as the time he went skinny-dipping after midnight in the Kinsey Park swimming pool with about a dozen other teenagers—of both sexes, would you believe it?—and when a police cruiser rolled up with a probing searchlight, they all scampered buck naked across the park and wound up in her kitchen, still dripping, and she gave them towels and blankets to wrap up in, then fed them hot cocoa with marshmallows. "Oh, your father could be unruly in those days," said Granny Mills. She pretended to be scandalized by this tale, but the children knew better, for she told it often, smiling as she clucked her tongue at such mischief.

What the yellowed clippings from the newspaper did not record about the championship match with Butch Hawkins was the moment Gordon recalled most vividly, when he first laid eyes on the girl who would become his wife. Unlike most of his matches, which he usually won in the first or second period with a pin, this one ran into the third round with the score tied, and the final seconds were ticking away when he gave one last heave, tipped Butch off balance, and threw him on the mat for a takedown. The Limestone South fans leaped to their feet and cheered, Pappy Mills loudest of all. Gordon and Butch stood apart, gasping for breath, then shook hands, and the referee lifted Gordon's arm. Sweaty, wrung out, he looked over the crowd, feeling about as much pride as a body could hold without bursting; then his gaze lit upon the face of Butch's little sister, who sat in the front row with her eyes squeezed shut and tears running down her cheeks.

"There I was, feeling on top of the world," Gordon would say when he came to this part of the story, "and there she was, bawling her eyes out. And it just took all the swell out of me."

"I was only twelve, but I wasn't a crybaby," Mabel pointed out, "and I didn't give a hoot about wrestling, but I adored my brothers, and here they'd both lost to this bully Gordon Mills. I shut my eyes and hoped he'd be gone when I opened them, and I'd never have to see him again."

Mabel did see him again, of course, or there wouldn't have been any Mills kids to learn this story. Here is how the reunion came about.

Seven years had passed since the wrestling match. Mabel was nineteen, a year out of high school, living with her parents and working in the Hoosier Hills Community Kitchen while trying to figure out what to do with her life. One spring evening, she was driving home from work along the highway in the rattletrap minivan her father kept around for hauling stuff, when the steering wheel suddenly jerked in her hands, and with a metallic screech the van swerved onto the berm, where she slowed to a stop. She turned off the engine, clicked on the flashing hazard lights, and waited for her heart to quit racing. Then she climbed out, walked around the nose of the van, and saw that the right front tire had blown. Like the other three tires, and like the spare she found under the cargo lid, it was as bald as her father's head.

Her father came to mind because he had taught her how to change a tire, back when she was learning to drive and before his heart attack put an end to such lessons. She remembered all the steps, but she got stuck on the first one, which was removing the lug nuts from the wheel. No matter how hard she pressed on the wrench, she couldn't loosen the nuts, not even when she stomped on the handle. She was no weakling, she wanted her kids to know, but she weighed only about half as much as either of her brothers, who would have been of some use right then. But after high school, Sonny and Butch had moved to Alaska, where they worked as bush pilots and salmon fishermen and fire-jumpers. They called home once every other month or so to brag about their adventures, but they never came back for a visit, not even after the heart attack laid their father low. They counted on Mabel to stay and look after the old folks, which of course she did.

Now came the part of the story that always made the Mills children shiver.

Dark was coming on. Cars and trucks whizzed by with their headlights blazing, nobody slowing down. If she had one of those cell phones like rich folks had, she could have called her dad to come pick her up. Sure, and if she had wings, she could fly. Maybe a state trooper would show up, or maybe some creep. As she waited, worrying, it began to rain—not hard, just enough to wet the pavement and make the other drivers rushing by even more reluctant to stop. Taking the lug wrench with her as a precaution, she climbed back into the driver's seat and watched the red streaks of taillights pulling away. After a while, as the drizzle turned to a hard rain, one set of taillights pulled over and came to a stop in front of the van. It was a rusty pickup loaded with barrels, not the sort of vehicle a nice, safe, older man or woman with a cell phone might drive. The door of the pickup opened, and out stepped a very large man—

"It's Pops!" Danny liked to shout at this point in the story, just to calm his nerves.

"Not yet," Mabel would remind him, "not by a long shot."

—out stepped a very large man—not tall, but wide, like her brothers, and he walked toward the van through the rain without a jacket or hat. His scalp gleamed from a buzz cut, so she guessed he was military, and young, from the swaggering way he moved. As he approached, she locked the doors and pulled the lug wrench from the passenger seat into her lap. She waited, heart pounding. Then she caught a glimpse of his face in the flashing amber glow of the hazard lights, and her fear gave way to relief, which gave way to irritation. Of all the men who might show up to help her out of a fix, why did it have to be the guy who beat her brothers?

Danny couldn't resist crying out, "I told you it was Pops!"

It was Gordon Mills, all right, but seven years older than when Mabel had last seen him, grinning at the center of the wrestling mat with his arm lifted in triumph. All she'd heard about him during those years was that his father had died in some kind of accident, and Gordon had quit high school and joined the navy and gone overseas. Running away, she thought, just like her brothers.

"He sent money home to Granny Mills," Veronica would remind everybody, "and he came to see her whenever he got leave."

"True," Mabel admitted. "But I didn't know that yet."

What Mabel knew back then, sitting in her van with the rain pouring down, was that she didn't have to like Gordon in order to lower the window and say yes when he asked if he could lend her a hand. She realized he didn't know who she was—

"Because you'd changed so much," Bruce put in.

"Yes, I'd changed a lot since I was that bawling twelve-year-old," Mabel agreed. "So far as he knew, he was helping a stranger, and that made me like him just a little bit."

Mabel started liking him a bit more when he asked if she could let go of that tire iron long enough for him to change her flat, and she liked him even more after she gave him the wrench and he insisted she stay in the van while he worked in the rain. He finished the job faster than she would have thought possible; then he wiped the jack and wrench with a rag from the cargo bin and stowed everything in back. By then, she trusted him enough to accept his offer to follow her home to make sure that bald spare didn't blow, and she liked him enough to feel a bit disappointed when they pulled up in front of her house and instead of sticking around to accept her thanks, he tooted his horn and drove off.

"The next day your mom called his mom!" Jeanne sang out, for she delighted in this part of the story.

Mabel always smiled, as she remembered the two mothers, who knew one another through the Limestone Quilters Guild, chatting away for several minutes about how frightening it must have been for a young woman to go careening off the road with a flat tire, Lord have mercy, the sky pitch-black, rain coming down in buckets, and traffic booming past, and how lucky it was that just the right young man happened by to help, a meeting surely designed by Providence to cure the young woman of a long-held grudge and to relieve the young man of long-held guilt. Mabel could almost hear violins playing in the background. Having thus framed the situation, the two mothers put their respective, and reluctant, offspring on the line.

In the ensuing conversation, Gordon learned that the pretty woman whose tire he had changed was the little sister of Sonny and Butch Hawkins, all grown up, and Mabel learned that the bully who defeated her brothers had mustered out of the navy in order to come home and look after his mother, who had been struggling to manage since his father's death. Mabel also heard from Gordon that the memory of her weeping face came to him every time he saw girls and women wailing during his tours in the Middle East, and such wailing happened often, whenever bombs demolished a house, or a child died in a crossfire, or a brother or husband or father was seized by fighters from one or another side in those never-ending wars. One thing he learned over there, he said, was that in war, unlike sports, everybody lost.

They talked long enough for Gordon to admit he was spooked by phones, so could they maybe go for a walk some time, or get some new tires for the van, or make popcorn and play euchre, or whatever it was that people did on dates? Mabel laughed at his notions; then Gordon let loose a roaring laugh, a huge, happy sound that poured through the telephone line into her ear.

When this story was retold in the twenty-fifth year of Mabel and Gordon's marriage, on a Sunday afternoon while all nine members of the household sat around the dining table savoring rhubarb-and-strawberry pie, Danny asked Mamaw Hawkins if Pops was his mommy's first boyfriend.

"Good gracious, no," Mamaw answered. "Boys positively swarmed around your mother, smart young beauty that she was, but she wouldn't take up with any of them because they had only one thing on their mind."

"What was that, Mamaw?"

"You'll find out soon enough."

"Did Pops have it on his mind?"

Mamaw Hawkins glanced at Gordon, who was studying a forkful of pie. "Oh, I expect so," she said, then quickly added, "but he was also thinking about other things, like helping Granny Mills and working overtime at the city garage so he could save money to buy a house."

"Our house," said Danny.

"Yes, this very house."

"He fixes it," said Danny.

"Yes, he does. He's handy. Your mother could see that by how fast he changed the tire in a storm. And when he started courting her, she saw he also has pluck, the deep-down strength you can draw on when you're in a hard place, the kind that keeps you from losing your way."

"And that's why I fell for the big galoot," Mabel said, patting Gordon's bearded cheek. "Pluck, and his good looks."

"And that's why I'm here," said Danny, who understood that parents fall in love and then children come along, although he did not yet grasp, as Veronica, Bruce, and Jeanne did, how love and babies are connected, or how improbable it is that any two people manage not only to find one another among the millions of possible partners but to stay together for a quarter century.

Widows

As old men died off in Gordon's neighborhood, the number of widows grew. Whenever he saw one of these women shoveling snow or lugging a trash can to the curb or struggling to start a car, he thought of his own mother, who'd been a widow for over thirty years. If she weren't living under his roof, how would she manage? Some of the neighborhood widows had sons or daughters who stopped by to check on them, but others seemed to be all on their own. Naturally, when Gordon spied one of the lonesome ladies changing the storm windows or cleaning the gutters or doing any other job she had no business doing, he would go lend a hand.

"If you play handyman for every woman in town who's lost her husband," Mabel complained to him one Saturday, "you'll make a widow out of me."

"Well, you're bound to be one sooner or later," Gordon replied.

"I'd rather it be later," Mabel said. "I don't want you keeling over just as I'm about to get you civilized."

Gordon knew this was Mabel's rough way of saying she loved him. She had gentler ways of saying it, but she wasn't in the mood to use them just then because he had neglected his chores at home half the day while helping three widows.

He'd begun the morning dutifully, shutting off the main water valve to the house so he could repair the dripping kitchen faucet. But no sooner had he dismantled the faucet than he noticed Mrs. Westover across the street digging in her flower bed. A small woman, she was so light she couldn't push the shovel into the soil with one foot, and when she tried pressing with both feet, she tipped sideways onto the lawn. Gordon hurried over to see if she'd broken any bones.

"Right as rain," Mrs. Westover announced as she dusted herself off. "But that ground gets harder every year, and here I am with a whole sack of gladiola bulbs."

"Let me see what I can do," Gordon said, taking up the shovel. He soon had the dirt loosened up, but before he could wish Mrs. Westover a good day and return to finish work on the faucet, she asked in her shaky voice if he would be so kind as to help her plant the gladiolas. What else could he do but agree? There were fifty bulbs, and Mrs. Westover was particular about how they were placed, so it took the better part of an hour. Just as he was covering the last one, he caught the glint of a cat's-eye marble in the black soil. He picked it up, rubbed it clean, and cupped it in his palm to show the old woman.

"Ah," she said wistfully, "that would be one of Joshua's. He played marbles all over this yard with his buddies."

Knowing that Joshua, her only child, had been killed in Vietnam, Gordon felt bad about turning up this reminder, so he closed his fist around the hard glass ball.

"Many a time," Mrs. Westover continued, "I'd look out and see the boys down on their knees in the grass, hunched over, lining up their shots." She sighed. "I don't see children doing that anymore. They won't bother with anything that doesn't require batteries."

"Danny must be a throwback," Gordon said, "because he still collects marbles. He keeps them in a jar on his windowsill, to catch the sunlight."

"Is that so?" The old woman tapped her chin thoughtfully, spun around, and bustled into the garage, calling over her shoulder, "Stay right there."

Presently she returned carrying a drawstring pouch. "These were Joshua's favorites," she said, "the ones he wouldn't risk losing in a game. Keepers, he called them. Perhaps Danny will add them to his collection."

Gordon thanked her, tucked the lumpy bag in his pocket, and hurried back toward his house, where his two daughters would be waiting for their morning showers, the grandparents would be craving their coffee, and Mabel would be itching to start the laundry. If he didn't get the water flowing again soon, the whole family would be up in arms. He was nearing the kitchen door when he heard a cry of alarm, which came from two houses down, where he saw the widow Mrs. Hernandez clinging to the top of a stepladder on her front porch.

Gordon took off running and arrived just in time to brace the teetering ladder and ease the old woman down. She blinked her gray, nearly blind eyes at him. "Saints in heaven," she said, patting her bosom, "my balance isn't what it used to be."

Peering into the rafters under the porch roof, Gordon asked, "What were you looking for, Mrs. Hernandez?"

"I'm worried the robin's nest is going to fall." She pointed at a grassy cup resting on one of the rafters. "I believe there's eggs inside, but I got dizzy before I could see to make sure."

"Let me have a look." Gordon climbed the ladder, peeked in the nest, and counted five bright-blue eggs, each one not much larger than the marble he'd found in Mrs. Westover's flower bed.

"Five!" Mrs. Hernandez exclaimed. "The mama has been busy. But I wish she'd find a safer location for her nest. Last year it fell down before the chicks fledged, and the cats made a meal of them. What do you think?" she asked Gordon. "Does that nest look secure to you? Perhaps you could build a little shelf?"

He thought of the faucet parts laid out on a sheet of newspaper beside the kitchen sink, his family waiting for water. But here was Mrs. Hernandez, her husband gone less than a year, her eyes failing, worried about a batch of birds. So he said, "I bet I could rig up something."

"That's just what Miguel would have said. I suspect you'll find everything you need on his workbench. I haven't been able to go near it since he passed."

As she predicted, on the workbench in the garage where Mr. Hernandez had tinkered at various failed inventions as long as Gordon had known him, there were tools, screws, and scraps of wood. After another trip up and down the ladder for measurements, Gordon constructed a snug platform with a raised lip on all four sides, sanded it smooth so the birds wouldn't catch any splinters, and fastened it to the rafter.

He was reaching for the nest when Mrs. Hernandez cried, "Don't touch it with your hands! I'll get you a spatula, so your smell won't scare Mama Robin." She ducked through the front door, then popped her head back out to add, "Of course, I don't mean your smell in particular, Mr. Mills."

As he waited, Gordon reassembled the faucet in his head, fitting the new gaskets and O-rings just so. It would take him only a few minutes, once he got back home, to put everything together and open the main valve.

More than a few minutes passed before Mrs. Hernandez emerged from the house with a spatula. "I hunted high and low," she explained, "before I thought to look in the pressure cooker. How it got in there is beyond me."

"Things do have a way of wandering," Gordon said to spare her embarrassment. He knew from observing his mother and Mabel's parents how every sort of order breaks down as you age. If he and Mabel lived long enough, they would lose track of things, too.

With great care, mindful of those five blue eggs, he slid the spatula under the grassy cup and eased the nest onto the platform.

Mrs. Hernandez clapped. "Bravo! I can't thank you enough."

"The only thanks I need," Gordon said, "is you promising to call me before getting on a ladder again. If I'm not home, one of the kids will come."

"Oh, those kids! How I've enjoyed watching them grow. They're bigger every time I see them, like stalks of corn." She rubbed her forehead, as if trying to clear a fogged window. "Now, this is silly, but I've forgotten your younger daughter's name."

That green-eyed daughter rose up in Gordon's mind, dressed in her bathrobe, moaning for a shower. "You mean Veronica."

"Ah, yes. What a beauty! Is she still interested in birds?"

"She's nuts about them. She's got a feeder right outside her window, and she can name every kind that comes by."

"Does she have binoculars?"

Gordon folded the stepladder, considering how to answer without sounding poor. "No," he said, "but she's got braces on her teeth."

"Well, then, you stay here for just a minute."

She limped indoors. Gordon carried the ladder into the garage, and while he was in there, he put away the tools he had used and straightened up the workbench. As he came back out, a robin glided under the porch roof and settled into the nest. Good for her, he thought. Mama bird doing her job. He paused on the front walk and cast a guilty look up the street toward his house. He could almost hear the rising grumbles. Eventually Mrs. Hernandez reappeared, holding a small pair of binoculars by the strap. "Here you go," she said.

He lifted his palms toward her. "Now, Mrs. Hernandez, you'd better hang on to those."

"Nonsense. They're no earthly use to me, with my bad eyes. They were Miguel's, and nothing would tickle him more than to look down from heaven and see your pretty Veronica gazing through his binoculars at birds."

Hearing her delight, he accepted the gift, took his leave, and headed home, vowing to answer no more cries of alarm before marching into the kitchen, fixing that faucet, and turning the water back on. But along the way he passed the house of Mrs. McEwen, and there in the driveway stood the hefty widow herself, straddling a fallen tree branch and gripping a hatchet in both hands. Stopped in his tracks, he watched her lift the hatchet above her head and sway side to side as if trying to get a bead on the wood around the bulge of her stomach. Oh, Lord, he thought, she'll chop off her foot for sure.

"Whoa, there, Mrs. McEwen!" he yelled.

She lowered the hatchet, and her face brightened. "Why, Gordon, fancy you turning up. My silver maple dropped this giant limb, you see, and it's too heavy to budge, and it's got my car trapped, and me with a chiropractor's appointment, so when I couldn't get the chainsaw started, I grabbed the hatchet, but I can't see where to chop."

The image of Mrs. McEwen running a chainsaw made Gordon's scalp tingle. "Maybe I can move it off the drive and come back to cut it up later," he suggested. "Why don't you put away your tommyhawk and let me see what I can do?"

She did as he asked and then settled in a lawn chair to watch. Meanwhile, Gordon laid the binoculars and marbles out of harm's way, limbered up his legs, and apologized to his tricky back. Then he squatted over the butt end of the branch, worked his hands underneath, gave a grunt, and lifted. Mrs. McEwen cheered as he staggered backward, dragging the branch off the driveway and onto the grass.

"There, now," he said, straightening up and pressing a hand against his spine, "you can go on to the chiropractor's."

"Oh," she said, "that's not till next week."

"Next week?"

"I didn't know how long it would take me to clear a path for my car, so I figured I'd better make a start."

"Well," Gordon said, "I'll come back to cut this up and stack it for firewood some evening soon. Right now I've got to scoot on home."

"Before you go," Mrs. McEwen put in, "could you figure out why my furnace won't come on?"

He noticed for the first time that she was wearing several layers of sweaters, which added to her bulk. "Maybe the thermostat's set too low," he suggested.

"That was Riley's department. I haven't touched it since he died."

"Maybe the pilot light is out."

She frowned. "What's a pilot light?"

Patience, Gordon told himself. You can't leave an old lady in the cold. Helping her search through kitchen drawers, eventually he turned up a flashlight that worked and a box of matches. She stood at the top of the stairs as he descended into the basement, where he found an ancient gas furnace. To check the pilot light, he had to remove the front panel, lie down on the floor among dead crickets, and paw his way through cobwebs. Sure enough, there was no tiny blue flame. He relit it with a match, and the furnace burst into life, triggering the blower, which quickly filled the air with ageless dust. He coughed as he replaced the panel and climbed the stairs, wincing at the pain in his knees.

"Now I'll be toasty," Mrs. McEwen declared, wrapping him in her arms and kissing him on the cheek.

After disentangling himself, he said, "If it goes out again, you give a call."

"That reminds me," she said. "I was meaning to call you after I read in the paper about your older boy winning a chess tournament."

Pride kept Gordon from fleeing just yet. "That's our Bruce. He's a whiz at it. Captain of his high school team."

"Well, I have a little something for him," she said and waddled off down the hall. Sounds of rummaging emerged from one bedroom and then another before she returned bearing a small wooden box. "These are Riley's chess pieces. He loved to play, but I never learned. It all seemed so medieval to me, with its kings and queens and knights and castles. He'd be pleased to know they made their way to Bruce."

By now, Gordon had learned not to challenge widows who wished to bestow gifts. So he thanked her, tucked the box under one arm, backed away, and took off, pausing in the front yard only long enough to retrieve the marbles and binoculars. He trotted the whole way home, arriving out of breath in the kitchen, where Mabel greeted him with a look spelling several kinds of trouble. She noted once more through gritted teeth that he was going to make a widow out of her if he kept waiting hand and foot on every woman in town who'd lost a husband. Gordon tried joshing her into a better mood, but that didn't work. So he pulled out the gifts he'd brought home for the children, and the storm began to clear from her face.

Later, he would present the marbles to Danny, the binoculars to Veronica, and the chess pieces to Bruce. But first he put the faucet together while Mabel kneaded bread dough on the counter nearby. Then he went down to the basement, turned on the main water valve, causing the pipes to clatter, and clumped back up to the kitchen where he tested the faucet, which didn't leak a drop. He had escaped from the widows today before receiving a gift for his oldest child, so he shouted up the stairs, "Jeanne gets first dibs on the shower!" Soon there was coffee perking, which drew the grandparents from their various pastimes, and toilets were flushing, the washing machine was sloshing, and the water heater was burbling. It all sounded like music to Gordon.

"I don't begrudge you helping widows," Mabel confessed to him that night in bed as she rubbed his back. "It's just that if I live to be an old woman, I want you to still be around and kicking."

Gordon had just enough oomph left to nudge her leg with his toe, and then he plunged into sleep.

Smoke

*I*n Limestone, and in just about anyplace else in Indiana, if
you want to get elected to public office, you promise to cut
taxes, since Hoosiers generally believe that a cheap government is less of a nuisance than an expensive one. Give bureaucrats too
much money and they'll hire somebody to check up on your table man-
ners and inspect the locks on your gun cases. So long as water comes
out of the faucet when you turn on the tap, and what you flush down
the toilet disappears, and cops keep the streets safe, and teachers tame
the kids, what else do you need government for?

In light of that philosophy, you can understand why a candidate
hoping to unseat the mayor of Limestone ran on the slogan "Cut Out
the Fat!" and vowed to slice 10 percent from the city budget. The mayor
countered by vowing to cut 15 percent. The challenger upped his bid
to 20. By election day, the two were pledging to whittle away not only
every ounce of fat from the budget but also a fair amount of gristle and
bone. The mayor won and left it to the city council to figure out how to
fulfill his campaign promise.

The budget whittling soon reached the city maintenance department, prompting the supervisor to call Gordon Mills one April morning to deliver the bad news.

"Furloughed?" said Gordon, who was packing his lunch pail. "You mean laid off?"

"Furloughed is what we call it these days," said the supervisor. "Sounds nicer. It means you've still got a job, but you don't get a paycheck."

"Can I cash in those nice feelings at the bank?"

"Don't take it hard, Mills. They'll restore the funding when rats start breeding in the piles of trash nobody's picking up, and the potholes nobody's filling break a few axles on those shiny new trucks the weekend cowboys buy with money they're not paying in taxes. Then we'll call you to work. For now, kick back and relax, collect those unemployment checks, watch some hoops on TV, or go fishing."

Gordon had been laid off before, but he'd never accepted pay for loafing, and he wasn't about to start now. What would his kids think, with Dad home on a weekday? What he'd learned from his father and the other men he'd known while growing up is that you work until your body gives out, and then you get old and die. So he finished packing his lunch pail, grabbed his welder's gear, and drove to the college football stadium, where new grandstands were slowly rising. The contractor, who was months behind schedule on the project, sent him straight to join the construction crew. So by seven a.m., his usual hour for clocking in at the maintenance shop, Gordon was a hundred feet up, strapped into a body harness, welding joints on girders that would eventually support skyboxes for fat cats.

Whenever he worked high steel, Gordon could be thankful he was built like a troll, as his kids liked to point out—a mass of muscle on a squat frame, with feet as wide as a skillet. He didn't tip over easily, as his wrestling opponents had discovered back in school days. Still, he felt queasy while shuffling along narrow I beams, glancing down at rooftops and pavement and the swooping flights of birds. Even from twenty feet up, let alone a hundred, a slip could turn a body into a sack of bones if your harness failed. He knew four men who'd suffered that bad luck. The two who survived might have been the unluckiest—broken, patched up, barely able to creep about, like jalopies repaired with junkyard parts. They fed their families on disability checks. Gordon couldn't imagine liking the taste of food he hadn't sweated for. When he visited the survivors, he could never bring himself to ask them how it felt to fall. Had it been pure fear all the way down? Or had they felt an instant of relief before they hit the ground, knowing they would never have to sweat or freeze on high steel ever again?

The work was dangerous any time of year, but for Gordon it was most risky in spring, when flowers and women stirred from their winter drowse. Even through the stink of acetylene and boiling metal, he could smell the perfume of hyacinths and lilacs, and even with his welder's visor lowered, whenever he looked away from the blue flame of the torch, he could see the gleaming arms and legs and flowing hair of women as they emerged from winter's wraps, the dog walkers in dresses, the joggers in shorts, the strollers in tights, the cheerleaders practicing their routines down below in the stadium parking lot.

Mabel knew that April and May were the lethal months, because in the season of lilacs, she could smell on his clothes the odor of burnt matches, which lingered on his skin even after he showered. The smell brought back the delirium of their courtship from years earlier. She marked the beginning of that courtship from the time she was stranded beside the road with a flat tire and Gordon stopped to help. Fresh out of the navy then, with a wrestler's build that strained the buttons on his shirt, he gave off a whiff of sulfur as he jacked up the car and changed the tire. From the smell, she assumed he was a smoker. But he never touched a cigarette, pipe, or cigar. Only after their first date, which they spent in her parents' garage while he tuned up her old Honda, did she realize that Gordon himself was the smoldering match, and she was the friction that ignited him.

Now a few months shy of fifty, his thermostat turned several degrees cooler, Gordon usually carried about him only the sweet pungency of sweat. So when he smelled of sulfur, as he did now after beginning work at the stadium, Mabel kissed him firmly and gave him an extra warning as he left the house: "Watch your step, you old goat, and keep your mind on your business. I want you to come home in one piece, with your heart still inside your ribs."

To protect himself from sparks and molten metal, Gordon had to keep bundled up. No matter how hot the day, he wore boots the size of bread loaves, cowhide pants with reinforced knees, long-sleeved shirts of heavy green twill, an engineer's cloth cap, the welder's helmet, and elbow-length leather gloves—all to guard himself against flame and molten metal. And still he burned himself. His forearms were lumpy with scars. Old burns on his legs formed clearings in the thicket of midnight hair. On the rare occasions when his kids persuaded him to put on swim trunks and go with them to the city pool or Lake Debs, his blotched limbs unsettled other bathers, who thought he must have an exotic disease.

Other men on the crew could take off their shirts as the weather warmed. Soon the White guys changed from oatmeal to roasted peanut, the Asians turned caramel, the Black guys changed from chocolate to licorice. How was it, Gordon often wondered as he welded trusses, that all this male flesh could not hold his eyes, while the mere glimpse of a woman's wrist as she checked her watch or the flicker of ankles in high heels could make him sway? He never catcalled and whistled along with the other guys. With two daughters of his own, who seemed to him God's own lovelies, and a wife who grew prettier every year, he didn't want any girl or woman to feel she had to hide her beauty for fear of wolves.

In spring, Gordon could fall in love with women glimpsed on street corners during the time it took for a red light to turn green. He would notice a mane of wavy red hair, lips the pale pink of quince blossoms, the velvet shadow at the base of a throat, a creamy calf exposed beneath the hem of a dress. He would gaze at them sidelong out of his squat homeliness, never expecting so much as a glance in return, for Mabel and his mother and his daughters were the only women or girls who ever looked at him squarely without shying away. When the green light flashed and the women pursued their various paths, Gordon slouched off toward new infatuations.

He supposed it was lust, this fire that flared up in an instant. It was as though a pilot light had been lit in him around the age of twelve and had been burning ever since. All this turmoil was to ensure the perpetuation of the species, according to the high school health teacher, who hadn't offered further details. Gordon had done his part for the species, he supposed, maybe even a bit more than his part, by fathering four children who lived and two who were miscarried. But what was he to do with his desire now since Mabel had closed up shop in the baby business?

One spring day a few years earlier, Gordon and Bruce, then age twelve, were playing catch in the park when the boy asked him for the lowdown on sex.

"No offense, Dad," Bruce said, "but I'm feeling left in the dark on this, you know? Don't you want to fill me in before I get it from the web?"

"Sex?" Gordon pronounced the word as though it were the name of a distant country he knew by rumor but had never visited. He glanced around at the people sunning or strolling nearby who could overhear any words he might offer. So instead of answering, he stuffed his hand into the catcher's mitt and flipped the baseball to Bruce, then backed away, hoping to delay any talk about sex by opening a space too broad for anything but shouts.

Ignoring the listeners, Bruce shouted, "I figured out the mechanics, which are kind of gross!" He fired a pitch at Gordon, who was still backing away, hemming and hawing. "And I get the reproduction angle!"

They laced the air with their tosses, Bruce working on his curve, Gordon returning the ball with a snap throw from beside his ear.

The boy's voice rose among the calls of crows and shouts of kids. "I just don't see why it's such a big deal! Guys at school, it's all they want to talk about! So what's the secret?"

Gordon felt surrounded by attentive ears—sunbathers, couples knotted on blankets, Frisbee chasers, kite flyers, the feeders of sparrows and squirrels, the walkers of babies and dogs. He let Bruce's next pitch sail by to give himself time while fetching the ball to come up with an answer. The lowdown on sex? What's the secret? Gordon's own parents had never given him a clue on the subject. His father—having grown up on a farm, where studs and mares enacted the slam-bang of sex with the hasty, oversized gestures of cartoons—figured that Gordon could pick up the essentials by keeping his eyes peeled at the Indianapolis Zoo. Without ever having explained a thing, the old man died when Gordon was sixteen, simmering with desire, still clueless. His mother—wispy, frail, forever astonished by the muscular bulk of her lone child—recoiled from all signs of sex as though it were the slimy trail of a slug across her dinner plate. Even now, while she lived under his roof, she would cluck her tongue during TV movies when the hero and heroine kissed.

The baseball rolled to the feet of a young woman who was lounging on a bench near a hedge of forsythia. The woman's head was tilted back, eyes closed. Curly black hair fanned out across her shoulders. She wore a tank top the color of the forsythia blossoms and matching shorts, and her bare legs and arms were stretched out to catch the sun. Gordon approached her hesitantly. The ball lay nearly touching one of her feet, and he was uncertain how to retrieve it without scaring her.

He glanced back at Bruce, who was pounding a fist into his mitt, waiting for a throw, waiting for answers to his questions. In the sun, the straw-haired boy blazed with splendor, as though a constellation of fireflies had been spun into the shape of a child. Gordon found it hard to believe that any spark of this luminous boy had emerged from between his own thick, hairy legs. He waved his mitt, then turned back to the woman on the bench. How would it look, he wondered, if she were suddenly to open her eyes and find him looming there? Better warn her. Still dressed as he had come from work, except for the helmet and gloves, he lifted his red polka-dot engineer's cap and said to the woman, "Miss? Miss?"

Her eyes sprang open, then narrowed to a wary slit. What she saw, silhouetted against the sun, was a bull reared on its hind legs, and what she heard was a gruff "Kiss! Kiss!" She drew in a breath to scream but paused, noticing that the bull's foreleg pointed at the ground near her feet, where she saw a golden egg. She blinked, and the egg changed into a baseball, its cover scuffed like the leather of old shoes, and the bull changed into a husky old guy with a beard. Relaxing, she pushed the ball toward him with her toe and flashed him a smile.

Watching, at first Bruce saw only his father's burly shoulders soaking up time. Then it struck him that much more of the lady was outside her clothes than inside. As she moved, her breasts jostled beneath her shirt like a pair of kittens under a sheet. Suddenly he became intensely curious about kittens. The way light slicked off her legs made a fish whirl in his belly. Before this moment he had never suspected there was a pool in his belly, let alone a fish.

Gordon lowered the cap to his head and bent down to grab the ball. From this close, the woman smelled of mock orange and coconut oil. Her black hair gleamed in the sunlight. Flames began to lick the inside of his skull. Ears burning and sweat running down his neck, he meant to apologize for startling her, but his tongue wouldn't form the words. Unable to speak, he turned away and pegged a throw at Bruce. Then he staggered back toward his son, glad of the broad earth beneath his boots. An I beam wouldn't have been wide enough to hold him upright.

Puzzling over the secret pool and the muscled wheeling fish, Bruce came running up to meet him. "Hey, Pops, you all right?'

"A bit woozy," said Gordon.

"There's smoke coming off your head!"

"It does that. Don't worry. It'll pass."

"Your hat's on fire!" Bruce snatched off the polka-dot cap and threw it to the ground and stomped on it.

Gordon's head continued to smoke.

"It's your hair!" the boy cried. Quickly he folded his mitt and smacked Gordon on the skull.

The pummeling began to clear Gordon's head, but failed to quench the fire. "I'm okay," he muttered, ducking away from the next blow. He picked up the cap and mashed it back in place. "I just get a little over-heated sometimes. Too much sun."

"We better go home and get you an ice pack!" Bruce led the way, swiveling back every few steps to check on him.

Smoke seeped out from under the brim of Gordon's cap. It was the affliction he had known since he was Bruce's age. His mother, alarmed by these adolescent fevers, had taken him to the family doctor, who assured her that Gordon would suffer nothing worse than embarrassment from his telltale smoke, for he was as healthy as a horse, so healthy indeed that nature might have furnished this fiery signal as a warning to girls. Besides, the doctor concluded with a sigh, the boy would soon enough grow out of his fiery passion.

Bruce asked no more questions on the way home from the park, suspecting that the steamy cloud about his father's head and the fish wheeling in his own gut were the beginnings of an answer.

When father and son arrived at the house, Mabel took one sniff at her husband and exclaimed, "You old dog, you!" She led him by his meaty arm straight to the bathroom, where she helped him out of his clothes and turned on the shower to cold and shoved him in.

"If that doesn't do the job," Mabel called above the hiss of water, "I'll see what I can do at bedtime." She reached around the shower curtain and pinched his rump. "Right now I've got to fix supper."

Smoke

As Gordon soaked under the spray, he remembered his father's stories about fires in the underground coal mines of Indiana, fires that no amount of water could put out, fires that smoldered for years, for decades, beyond memory, smoke gathering in the tunnels until some crack in the earth released it in white billows to the sky. Gordon lathered his thinning hair, his grizzled beard, his chest, the rude companion between his legs. But neither soap nor shampoo could overpower the smell of sulfur. At bedtime he would be ready for Mabel. Shaking as always, nostrils full of her sweetness, he would teeter along the narrow girder, craving and dreading the plunge, high in the dangerous air.

Centaur

*L*imestone, Indiana, a city the mapmakers blithely ignore, is named for the bedrock on which it was built, a rock that formed on the bottom of an ancient sea as a hardened pudding of crushed shells. Just as water gives birth to limestone, so the rain and snowmelt that seep down from the surface slowly dissolve it, carving out sinkholes, tunnels, and chambers bristling with stalactites. The caves riddling the limestone under Limestone are not famous, like Mammoth or Carlsbad or Altamira, but what they lack in reputation they make up for in abundance, for they are as numerous as the air pockets in a loaf of sourdough bread. One of those caves deserves to be better known, maybe should even get written up in the road atlas, because for a while not long ago it was home to a herd of rare beasts.

There were bats, of course, and blind crayfish, eyeless salamanders, albino crickets, and shy spiders, the sorts of animals you might expect to find in any dark, dank grotto. But in addition, this cave provided refuge for a great many less common creatures, such as unicorns, griffins, dragons, and centaurs. Except for the phoenix, which was solitary, they all hung out in pairs—each satyr with a nymph, for example, and each harpy with a hippogriff. What they did in the dark was anyone's guess.

The mayor and city council planned to make the cave a tourist attraction as soon as the budget allowed them to pave a road to the entrance and build a gift shop. In the meantime, they kept the location a secret, so gawkers wouldn't go barging in and disturb the beasts. Aside from the mayor and council members, one of the few people who knew about the place was Gordon Mills, who, as part of his duties on the city maintenance crew, was ordered to install a gate of steel bars at the mouth of the cave and to clean the interior twice a year, in spring and fall. The bars allowed bats to fly in and out on their nightly errands, and a spare key, hanging from a hook just inside the gate, allowed the larger inhabitants to come and go as they pleased.

The cave was filthier in the spring, after the creatures had been cooped up inside all winter. Despite their horny scales and thick fur, they could not bear the cold, having evolved in warmer climes, so they ventured out mostly between April and October. Even in the warmer months, they didn't wander far, wishing to avoid encounters with dog walkers or mushroom hunters or wandering lovers who might sound the alarm and have them banished. The beasts had already fled from one country after another, scorned by skeptics or driven away by mobs. The cave harbored smells from the many places they had left—olive groves, peach orchards, marble quarries, mossy riverbanks, candlelit cathedrals, trash-strewn alleys, dusty libraries, and battlefields. Desperate to find a safe haven, they wound up in the backwoods of Indiana, where they hoped eventually to blend in with the local wildlife.

While cleaning the cave, Gordon learned all about their history and habits, mainly from the centaurs, who wanted to practice their English. They spoke with an accent, of course, being foreigners, but he could understand them well enough. They knew geography backward and forward, from all their wandering. Gordon had never heard of half the places they'd been kicked out of. From what the centaurs let slip about their escapades with women, he could see why folks might not welcome them in the neighborhood. He certainly wouldn't want them anywhere near his daughters.

The phoenix, who looked like a cross between a golden eagle and a turkey buzzard, only way bigger, had an accent so thick it took Gordon a while to figure out that she was asking him to borrow a match. He said he didn't have any on him because he didn't smoke. Maybe she'd never heard a Hoosier before because she just gave him a puzzled look and repeated the question. So he tried using hand motions, like in charades, pretending he was striking a match and smoking a cigarette and then drawing a big *X* in the air and shaking his head. But she only frowned. Next he flapped his arms for wings and puffed out his cheeks and blew hard, by way of saying she could ask one of the dragons for a light, a suggestion that made her shudder and nestle down on her pile of sticks.

Except for the unicorns, who batted their eyelashes at him and never made a sound, the other beasts all rattled on to him in their various languages as he worked. The satyrs sniggered, the nymphs hummed, the griffins snarled, and the dragons rumbled like distant thunder. From the few words Gordon could make out, they talked mostly about sex and food. Which, now that he thought about it, was mostly what the guys at the shop talked about, aside from sports and crops and dogs.

How the beasts paired up was a puzzle to him, but then how any two humans paired up was also a puzzle to him. Take his own marriage, for instance. Why would a woman as pretty and smart and tenderhearted as Mabel agree to marry a lug like him? And why would she stay married to him for twenty-five years? Whatever the reasons, he thanked his lucky stars.

How the beasts fed themselves was less mysterious, for he recognized in the cave litter the bones of deer, foxes, possums, raccoons, rabbits, squirrels, dogs, catfish, and cats, along with gnawed roots and corncobs and hanks of hay. Out of sympathy with other endangered species, the centaur explained, they didn't eat bats or salamanders or crayfish, nor did they dig up orchids or ginseng, but everything else was fair game, so to speak. Evidently the griffins were the best hunters, for they could fly like eagles and pounce like lions. For those who preferred their meat cooked, the dragons would roast it with their fiery breath. They all drank from the stream that flowed through the cave. Gordon drank there as well during his visits, from a spot that allowed him a closer look at the nymphs washing their long hair.

When he showed up for the semiannual cleaning, the beasts were polite, apologizing for the mess, standing aside to let him shovel and sweep, some even offering to help. He thanked them but went about his work alone, afraid one of them might strain a muscle or slip a disk and sue the city. Besides, if they were really so eager to help, they could have tidied up the place before he arrived. In spite of the heaped bones and corncobs and wisps of hay, there wasn't much manure, a fact explained by one of the centaurs as the result of a metabolism that turned most of what the creatures ate directly into dreams. Dreaming, in fact, was their major pastime, to make up, he supposed, for not having TV or the internet.

It so happened that Gordon was cleaning the cave one October day soon after his daughter Veronica, now twelve, had declared herself too old to go trick-or-treating. This left only Danny, youngest of the Mills brood, to roam the neighborhood in costume, ringing doorbells, holding out an open sack, while Gordon kept watch from the sidewalk to make sure nobody kidnapped his sweet son. Before too many more years, even Danny would graduate from make-believe, and then what excuse would there be for a dad to wander outdoors among the pirates, witches, and ghosts? The thought made Gordon glum. In order to explain his melancholy to the centaur, he first had to describe Halloween. While listening, the centaur shuffled his hooves on the stony floor of the cave and scratched the hair on his chest, as if lost in thought.

Later that week, on the night of Halloween, Gordon was returning home with Danny, whose sack was bulging with candy and whose homemade dinosaur outfit was coming apart at the seams. They were just within sight of the house when down the front walk came Veronica and the centaur, side by side, her hand resting on his back, their heads drawn together, whispering.

"Way cool!" Danny cried. "Look at that killer costume!"

Gordon looked, and kept looking, as his daughter and the centaur strolled into the pool of light under a streetlamp and on beyond into darkness, the murmur of their voices dwindling away.

Blues

Gordon rarely came down with the flu or colds, but once in a while, usually in the depths of winter, he came down with a severe case of sadness. When he suffered these dark bouts, Mabel would warn the family, "Careful, he's in the dumps." His beard, normally as black as used crankcase oil, would take on a bluish tinge in certain lights, prompting his children to say, "Dad's got the blues."

One Saturday morning in December, not long before Christmas, first Mabel, then the four children, and then the three grandparents all noticed that Gordon's whiskers had turned the color of an old bruise. This change alerted everyone in the Mills household to raise their voices when speaking to him, if they spoke to him at all, for sadness made him slightly deaf as well as cranky.

Sadness also enveloped him in a cloud of gloom that muffled his voice, blurred the outlines of his body, and felt dry and prickly to the touch. If Gordon could have said what his gloom felt like from inside, he might have compared himself to a bullfrog buried in the cracked bottom of a dried-up pond, hunkered down, waiting for rain. But he never spoke about his feelings. He accepted their comings and goings without surprise or complaint.

Mabel could guess at causes for his latest attack of sadness—bills piling up, appliances breaking down, dwindling daylight, lengthening nights, his joints aching as he worked outdoors on the city maintenance crew in the bitter cold. It didn't help that Jeanne had returned home from college for the holidays with her hair dyed green and the tattoo of a hummingbird on her ankle; or that their younger daughter, Veronica, all of twelve years old, had asked for a push-up training bra for Christmas; or that Bruce had fallen in love with a princess in a video game. As if those weren't enough reasons for feeling the blues, there were also Mabel's parents, who kept forgetting where they had put their Medicare cards or false teeth or other vital possessions, and Gordon's mother, who kept sneaking off to gamble away her social security check at the French Lick Casino.

Fortunately, Mabel herself never gave in to sadness. It was a luxury she couldn't afford. If she withdrew into a cloud of gloom, the Mills household would come apart at the seams. She couldn't even stay overnight at the annual quilters' retreat in Spring Mill State Park without returning home to find the place a shambles. Some people would call Gordon's glum mood a case of depression rather than sadness. But Mabel knew the difference. Depressed people lost all their zip. They lay around in the daytime with the shades drawn, or they sat in a chair staring at the wall, or they watched reruns on TV. Their beards didn't turn blue. They didn't get up from the breakfast table, as Gordon did this Saturday morning, and go out to the garage and overhaul a snowblower.

Mabel knew what he was up to in the garage, for she had opened the door to tell him she would feed him waffles, popcorn, and watermelon pickles for lunch. Ordinarily, the prospect of eating comfort foods would begin to scatter Gordon's gloom, the way sunlight melts away fog. But he merely continued probing the guts of the machine. So Mabel repeated the news, louder this time, adding Vienna sausages to the menu. When he still didn't reply, she sighed and returned to the kitchen. She had a household to run. He would get over his funk sooner or later.

Over the course of the morning, one member of the family after another ventured into the garage on a mission to cheer him up. Jeanne assured him that the green dye in her hair would wash out and that the hummingbird on her ankle was the only tattoo she planned to get. Bruce promised to break up with the video game princess as soon as he could find a new girlfriend online. Veronica, wishing to downplay her request for a push-up bra, mentioned other items she would love to find under the Christmas tree, including a bat house, which she just knew could be made by a certain clever daddy. Granny Mills reported that she had won almost as much money on the slot machines as she would have to pay for the speeding ticket she got on her drive to French Lick. At first, Mamaw and Papaw Hawkins forgot why they had gone out to the garage, but when they saw the bulky figure of their son-in-law wielding a wrench, they remembered they had come to rescue him from sadness. But then they forgot how they had planned to pull off the rescue, so they retreated to the kitchen, shaking their heads at Mabel when she glanced up from the counter, where she was stirring waffle batter.

After all of these visitors had failed to rouse any response from Gordon, Mabel began to fear that this bout of darkness might last through Christmas, casting a shadow over the festivities. Usually, at this time of year, Gordon would be holed up in the garage, humming some broken tune, making presents for everybody out of wood scraps and parts from defunct machines. Last Christmas, for example, he had made her an aluminum measuring cup out of an old carburetor. No amount of washing could remove the tang of gasoline, so she only used the cup when cooking a treat just for Gordon, such as these waffles, since he didn't seem to mind the taste. This year, instead of making presents, he was fixing that snowblower, silent as a stone, wrapped in the thickest coat of gloom she had ever seen him wear.

For a fleeting moment, Mabel thought maybe she should take a turn at being sad and let somebody else take charge for a while. Just then, Danny waltzed in, bright and beaming, like the first shaft of morning sunlight streaming into the kitchen. At seven, ginger-haired and green-eyed, he was still too young and uncorrupted by the world to come up with notions that might cause a parent to despair.

"Is the Tyrannosaurus rex still in the garage?" Danny asked.

"Yes," Mabel said, "but you shouldn't go out there. Daddy's not in the best of moods."

"He will be."

"Oh, will he?" She smiled at her son, whose face shone with excitement. "And why are you so sure you can cheer him up?"

"I've got a secret plan," Danny confided.

"Well, give it a try. If you can get him to growl at you, that would be an improvement. Right now, he's incommunicado."

"I thought he was in the garage."

"I mean he's not talking. So don't get your hopes up. While you're out there, be a sweetie and fetch me a bottle of watermelon pickles from the canning shelves. "

Danny opened the door to the garage and padded quietly toward the workbench, where his father, dimly visible through a murky cloud, was hunched over a burned-out snowblower that the two of them had picked up at the town dump last summer. The only sound was the tapping of a hammer against a seized-up bolt.

Danny crept forward, hands outstretched, until he felt the dry, bristly edge of the gloom. Raising his voice, he called, "Daddy, why did the chicken cross the road?" When no answer came, he said, "To boldly go where no chicken has gone before."

The hammer tapping paused, so Danny said, "Why did the hippo cross the road?"

From the gloom came a growl or maybe a snort.

"To visit the chicken," Danny said.

Another snort, louder this time.

"And why did the turkey cross the road?"

"I dunno," came the gravelly voice. "Why?"

"Because it was the chicken's day off."

A rumbling chuckle shook the air and rattled tools on the workbench. Danny pressed forward into the cloud of sadness, which now felt soft and moist on his cheeks. He could make out the gorilla shape of his father in the mist, with tiny sparks flickering all around in the fog, like fireflies.

Pursuing his plan, Danny said, "Knock, knock." He paused, then added, "Come on, Pops. You're supposed to say, 'Who's there?'"

"Okay. Who's there?"

"Bach."

"Bach who?"

"Bach, bach! I'm a chicken!"

His father guffawed.

Danny giggled. "Knock, knock."

"Who's there?"

"Cow go."

"Cow go who?"

"No, cow go MOOO!"

"Ha!"

"Knock, knock."

"Now who the devil's there?"

"Irish."

"Irish who?"

"Irish you a merry Christmas."

As more and more sparks shot through the damp cloud, Danny said, "Knock, knock."

"Who the dickens is it now?"

"Olive."

"Olive who?"

"Olive you, Pops."

Now the sparks turned into needles of light flashing through the gloom. They reminded Danny of the time he woke his daddy way early in the morning, before anyone else was up, and the two of them trooped down to the park and lay on the grass and his daddy drew him close with a big hairy arm and they watched meteors streak across the sky.

Here in the garage, those big arms once again drew Danny close, pulling him into the heart of the cloud, where lightning flared and thunder boomed and rain began to fall. It was a warm rain, the kind that brings tadpoles and tulips in spring. Danny tilted his face into the downpour, grinning up at his father, whose beard no longer showed a hint of blue.

Wealth

*H*ere it was, less than two weeks before Christmas, and the Mills household was flat broke. Gordon learned this fact at bedtime on Friday from Mabel, who kept the checkbook. She often delivered bad news during the brief interval between when Gordon's head hit the pillow and when he began to snore, since it offered a rare chance to unload her worries without other ears listening in. In the daytime, up to seven pairs of ears could listen in, so it was hard to keep anything secret once you said it aloud.

On Friday evenings, after a week of patching up streets and sewer pipes and other crumbling parts of the city, Gordon felt as if he had been pounded head to foot with a hammer. Sleep was the only relief. "Let's dip into savings," he suggested drowsily.

"We've already dipped in for Veronica's braces and Mamaw's new hip," Mabel reminded him. "There's zero in savings, and seven dollars in checking."

Gordon forced his eyes open and squinted into the glow of the reading lamp over Mabel's side of the bed. "Can't we borrow against my pension?"

"We borrowed up to the limit for Jeanne's tuition, and Lord knows how we'll pay for her next two years."

Giving up on sleep, Gordon started thinking about money, his least favorite subject. His paychecks never quite covered the family's expenses, which kept edging up with inflation, while his pay hadn't increased in five years due to a property tax freeze imposed by the stingy legislature. In the warmer months, he earned extra bucks in the evenings and on weekends by painting houses, cleaning gutters, laying bricks, trimming trees, or hauling stuff in his truck. In winter, it was too dark to work outdoors in the evening, and on weekends about all he could do was shovel snow. But recent winters had been so warm, they brought little snow, and what little they brought soon melted. So far this year, midway through December, not a flake had fallen in southern Indiana.

"You could murder me and collect the insurance," he said.

"I thought of that," Mabel said. "But the cops would catch me and send me to prison. Then who'd look after the kids and the grandparents?"

"I figured you'd have the perfect crime scoped out, with all the mysteries you read."

It was true that Mabel had a taste for novels featuring blood and corpses on their covers. Her current bedtime book was called *Yuletide Gore*, with a cover showing a body dressed up like Santa Claus laid out beneath a lit-up Christmas tree. She was a quarter of the way into the book, and still nobody had been murdered, so she couldn't begin to guess who the victim would be. But she was building up a list of potential murderers, beginning with a glamorous red-haired diva who played the piano and feigned holiday cheer but was clearly up to no good.

"Even if I could get away with bumping you off," Mabel said, "we'd spend all the insurance money on your funeral. No, no. I've invested too many years in civilizing you. I don't have the patience to train a new husband." She snuggled against him and twirled a finger in his chest hair, which was as wiry as steel wool. "Besides," she said, "I like having you around, even if we're broke."

Gordon laid his hand on top of hers, his palm as rough as a cheese grater. "We could skip presents this year," he said.

"I'm not even thinking about presents. I'm thinking about groceries. I wanted to stock up before the blizzard, but I knew the next check would bounce."

"There's a blizzard coming?"

"Six or eight inches by morning."

A grin split Gordon's black beard. "Then ease your mind, sweetums. We'll be flush again by tomorrow night."

When his wheezing turned to snores, Mabel slid her hand out from under his callused paw and resumed reading *Yuletide Gore*. The next suspicious character to enter the story was a rugged guy with a booming voice and killer good looks. He played the guitar and claimed to be a folksinger, but Mabel could tell he was something less wholesome—a junk bond salesman, maybe, or an actor.

Sure enough, by dawn on Saturday, when Gordon opened the garage door to step outside, the snow reached halfway up his high-top rubber boots. The storm had blown past, and the eastern sky was robin's-egg blue. His cheeks stung with cold. There would be no melting today. He should be able to earn a couple hundred bucks by nightfall, enough to fill the fridge and buy a few presents.

Without waiting for breakfast, he gassed up the snowblower. The machine had been a rusted hulk when he and Danny had salvaged it from the town dump back in the summer. Since then, with the boy watching his every move, Gordon had refurbished it piece by piece—rebuilding the engine, replacing the drive chain and auger, greasing the gears, painting the chassis catsup red—and now the juiced-up contraption gleamed.

Eager to see how it would perform in its first real test, he put on ear protectors, cranked the engine, set the augur spinning, and went roaring down the driveway, clearing a swath two feet wide. Snow streamed from the chute, light as feathers, forming a white veil as it fell to one side of his path. He continued on across the street to clear the front walk and driveway of the house belonging to Mrs. Westover, a retired librarian whose husband had recently died. When she appeared at the door holding her purse and waving at him, Gordon realized he couldn't accept money from a widow, so he waved back and chugged along the sidewalk.

He decided to clear snow for the other neighborhood widows first, and then he would move on to paying customers. So he proceeded to the home of Mrs. Hernandez, who flicked her Christmas tree lights off and on by way of thanks; then to the home of Mrs. McEwen, who blew him a kiss; and then to three other houses, always hurrying away before any of the women could offer him money.

Meanwhile, at her post in the kitchen, Mabel stole a few minutes between chores to read *Yuletide Gore*. Still no murdered Santa Claus, but a third suspect had appeared—a soft-spoken man who claimed to be a Quaker pastor, a champion of peace and kindness—surely one of the phoniest disguises she had ever come across in a mystery novel.

Thoughts of Gordon, out there in the cold earning money for the family, prompted her to close the book. She packed his lunch bucket with all the treats her depleted refrigerator and pantry could supply, and then she enlisted Danny to deliver it.

Gordon was finishing up the sidewalk for the last of the neighborhood widows when Danny came hustling along lugging the lunch bucket.

"Mom says you've got to eat because you're keeping bread on our table," Danny said.

While Gordon wolfed down an egg sandwich, a bagel with cream cheese, dill pickles, Vienna sausages, watermelon pickles, and a handful of chocolate chip cookies, Danny looked over the idling machine. "Can I drive it?" he asked.

"Sure, but only if you wear these." Gordon removed his orange ear protectors and fitted them over Danny's black knit cap.

"I bet I look like a bug," Danny said, patting his head. "But what'll you wear?"

"My hearing's already shot. I want to save yours."

With Danny walking between the handles, clinging to the rubber grips, and Gordon walking behind to guide the machine, they cleared snow at the house of the man who had taught all four Mills children in kindergarten, and naturally such a man could not be asked to pay, nor could the couple down the block who were expecting their first baby any day now, nor could the hairdresser whose daughter had leukemia, nor could the machinist who had lost his job, nor could the minister with the broken leg.

In fact, although the two of them kept plowing until sunset, Gordon couldn't bring himself to accept money from anyone, not even from strangers who came outside waving greenbacks and shouting thanks.

As they headed home, both encrusted in snow, Danny asked, "Where's the bread?"

"What bread?"

"For our table. Like Mom said."

Gordon was trying to think of an answer when Mrs. Westover toddled up, wearing her late husband's hunting coat and carrying a bundle wrapped in a pink dish towel. "Two loaves of whole wheat," she said, "just out of the oven."

Gordon took off his gloves to accept the bundle, which was still warm. Mrs. Westover patted his cheek, patted Danny's head, and then toddled away.

"Well, here's the bread," Danny said.

"I guess so," said Gordon, handing him the bundle. "Now run home and give it to Mom. Tell her I'll be along for supper as fast as this old machine and my gimpy legs can go."

When Danny burst into the kitchen, shedding snow on her freshly scrubbed floor, blurted his message, plopped the bread on the counter, and then rushed back outside, Mabel looked up in a daze from *Yuletide Gore*. To her disappointment, there was still no dead Santa, but a likely victim had just turned up. He was a retired English professor who wrote satirical sketches about the three suspicious characters and kept correcting their grammar, giving each of them ample motive to bump him off. She would have to wait until bedtime to discover who did him in.

She set Mrs. Westover's gift on the kitchen table beside those that had already arrived—a blueberry pie from Mrs. McEwen, a Three Kings fruitcake from Mrs. Hernandez, a plum pudding, two salads, three casseroles, canning jars filled with veggies and fruits, and enough other food to restock the pantry and refrigerator. The doorbell had been ringing all afternoon. It rang again now, and Mabel opened the door to find the children's kindergarten teacher, who presented her with a carton of eggs from his backyard chickens. As the teacher left, she was about to close the door when she spied Gordon trudging homeward, driving the bright-red snowblower, his beard shaggy with icicles, and three neighbors trailing him, each bearing a gift.

Maintenance

*G*ordon never used the telephone if he could avoid it. How could he tell for sure where the voice that slipped through the earpiece was coming from? It might sound like a fishing buddy calling from across town, but for all Gordon knew, it could be a stranger playing a trick, or a computer scheming to sell him a magazine subscription, or an alien astronaut radioing from the moon. And when his own words drained into those tiny holes in the mouthpiece, trembled along the web of wires, circled the globe under oceans, and bounced off satellites, how could anyone say where they would end up?

"It won't bite," his four children would tell him when the phone rang and Gordon flinched away.

All four of them would race to answer a ringing phone, hoping to find romance, fortune, or adventure pouring from the receiver. They would talk with anyone about anything—with salesmen about cemetery plots, with pollsters about toothpaste, with fundraisers about money, with wrong numbers about loneliness; they would even talk, so far as their knowledge permitted, with sex maniacs about anatomy.

Listening to their telephone chatter from behind the screen of his newspaper, Gordon was amazed that his offspring could speak with so much abandon over that terrifying instrument.

His children, his wife, and the three grandparents gave up trying to coax Gordon out of his phobia. They all shared the single push-button phone mounted on the kitchen wall because the household couldn't have afforded a cell phone without taking out a second mortgage. On the rare occasions when someone actually called for him, the family made up stories to explain why he was not available to talk. He's fishing, they might say, or he's running the table saw in the garage, or he's asleep in the hammock. Danny, the seven-year-old cutup, liked to say that his father was away on a journey—to Antarctica, maybe, on a hot day, or to Africa on a cold one.

Once Danny tried the Antarctica story on Gordon's boss, the supervisor of the city maintenance crew.

"Gone to the South Pole?" said the supervisor. "But I saw him at work this afternoon."

Without batting an eye, Danny explained that his daddy's trip to the bottom of the earth, while sudden, was also brief, and that reliable old Gordon Mills would show up for work as usual tomorrow morning at six o'clock sharp.

"Tell him not to come in until midnight," said the supervisor, "because I'm going to put him on a new job. You got that?"

"Roger," said the boy. "Over and out."

Rubbing his eyes to stay awake, Gordon trudged into the maintenance shop the following midnight. The supervisor greeted him with a hundred-watt smile. Because of Gordon's finicky back, which had been giving him a lot of trouble lately, the supervisor had pulled strings to get him off the street crew, with its jackhammers and shovels, and onto a desk job.

"Starting tonight, you're the dispatcher on the graveyard shift," said the supervisor. "Since nobody else is around after midnight, all you do is answer the phone, take messages, call up emergency crews. Easy as pie. Nothing to strain that old back."

"Hold on now," Gordon muttered.

The supervisor raised his palms. "No need to thank me. You're a blame good worker, Mills. You never complain, and you do whatever job I put you on, like cleaning out that cave and chasing alligators. So now I'm looking after you."

The supervisor took off. Gordon slumped into the dispatcher's chair. Minutes passed without a sound except the tick of diesel engines, hot from the day's chores, now cooling in the garage. Ordinarily at this hour, Gordon would have been deep in dream. But now he could scarcely blink, let alone sleep. The black telephone crouched on the desk in front of him like a panther about to spring. When it finally rang, he lurched in his chair. This was not the brassy ding of the phone at home, but more like a tornado siren or the screech of a fierce bird, a sound calculated to wake the most stubborn sleeper.

I could just quit and walk off the job, thought Gordon. But then who's going to pay for the notes on the house and car, the insurance, the dentist, the doctor, the grocer, the gas and electric, the charge card, the lottery tickets, the birdseed?

Screwing up his courage, as he used to do in the Seabees before climbing onto a bulldozer to smooth out another acre of desert in a country thick with snipers and buried explosives, Gordon picked up the phone on the seventh ring. "Maintenance," he said through clenched teeth.

"Just checking," said the supervisor, or at least it was a voice that sounded like the supervisor and declared itself to *be* the supervisor. How could you know for sure? "Everything okay, Mills?"

"Fine," said Gordon.

"Thatta boy. Now I'm going to catch a few Zs. The city is in your hands, Mills. Don't let it fall apart before morning."

Gordon hung up, encouraged by having survived one spring of the panther. He lined up the message pad and pencil on the right side of the phone, the list of emergency numbers on the left. Minutes passed in silence. He began to relax. Maybe no one else would call. Then suddenly the siren screech erupted again, and his heart thumped. This time he answered on the fifth ring. Before he could say "Maintenance," a man's drunken voice, with jukebox and clink of glass in the background, said, "Tell Mildred I'm sorry and won't ever do it again, and if she'll forgive me, I'll love her socks off just like in the old days. Otherwise, she can take a flying leap."

"What?" said Gordon.

"Don't play dumb with me," said the drunk. "Just write it down." The man slowly repeated his message, and Gordon wrote it on the pad.

Next a woman called to report that a burst water main was flooding her basement. At least this fell within Gordon's territory—assuming, of course, the woman was telling the truth.

"Ma'am," he said, "no offense, but how do I know you're not just making this up?"

"Listen," she replied, and through the earpiece came the sound of gurgling water.

"Begging your pardon, but how do I know that's not just a running faucet?"

The woman shrieked. Abandoning his questions, Gordon realized he would have to accept on faith whatever people told him over the phone, for there was no way he could reach through the wires and grab hold of truth.

"Okay, okay," he said. "Help is on the way." He dialed a plumber, who, though roused in the middle of the night, sounded cheerful at the prospect of earning double-time pay.

Three calls answered, one call made, and Gordon was still alive and kicking. This really wasn't so bad. He might survive until morning.

Soon, he was no longer twitching when the phone rang. He learned to pinch the receiver between shoulder and ear as he'd seen secretaries do, freeing both hands for messages. In rapid succession, he took down reports of broken windows, buzzing streetlights, a fallen flagpole, buckled sidewalks, stalled squad cars. Who would have thought so many things could go wrong in a sleeping city? But Gordon was up to it; for each emergency he gave advice or dispatched a crew.

Between calls, every now and again, into the quiet office, he whispered, "Maintenance."

As the night deepened, it seemed that not only the city was falling apart, but so were many of its citizens. A hysterical boy—or perhaps it was a girl—phoned to say that his (or her) cat was trapped in the chimney. To make matters worse, the cat was an albino and the chimney had not been cleaned in ages. "Call the fire department," said Gordon.

"*You* call them," pleaded the boy (or girl), "because I've got to keep an eye on my kitty."

Gordon called the fire department. In response to later pleas, he called the hospital, the Salvation Army, a psychiatrist, an all-night karate instructor, a tow truck, and a bookie. One lady begged for advice about the color of a new couch, and since there were no interior decorators open at that hour, Gordon told her, "Cigar brown." A man wanted to know what to buy on the futures market, and Gordon suggested pork bellies.

Why so many requests that had nothing to do with the crumbling fabric of the city? Gordon pulled the phone book from a desk drawer and found the maintenance shop listed on the inside cover, five lines below the police. Flustered and sleepy, meaning to call the ambulance, maybe, or the weather bureau, or the cops, people dialed him by mistake. Of course they might all have been pranksters, or computers, or actors on tape. The fact remained, however, that Gordon was equal to their needs, whether real or invented. Now, in the lull between calls, he found himself actually looking forward to the next ring.

"Maintenance," he declared, practicing in the silence.

In the phone book he noticed a few listings that aroused his curiosity. Dial-a-Poem, for example. When was the last time he'd listened to poetry? Probably eighth grade, when Mrs. Vickers recited verses by some English lady with three names. And how about the Abortion Help

Line? Mama Bear's Midnight Recipes? Stone Country Dating Service? The Hundredth Hill Music Camp?

Gordon Mills, a lifelong hater of telephones, discovered that his dialing finger itched. A private call or two wouldn't hurt, he figured, so long as he didn't tie up the line for long. First he dialed the poem, which turned out to be a jumble of words that didn't even rhyme, and then four prayers, including one from the Whirling Dervishes. Next he dialed up weather advice for overseas travelers and learned of a typhoon approaching Japan and a blizzard in Finland and monsoons in Sri Lanka. As soon as he hung up, the phone rang, and it was a furious woman demanding to know why she'd been getting a busy signal for an hour when her sports car was out in the drive smashed flat under one of the city's fallen oaks. "Were you gossiping with your floozy?" the woman demanded.

"I was listening to poetry and prayers," Gordon answered.

"Likely story. Poetry, my foot! I wasn't born yesterday, mister. You men are all alike. Take my ex, for instance. He had a little black book filled with the names and numbers of more floozies than you could shake a stick at." The voice paused, then shifted key. "Say, how old are you, anyway? You sound kind of cute."

Never one to say much, Gordon had scarcely thought about the sound of his voice and certainly never dreamed that a strange woman in the depths of the night would think of it as cute. "I'm married," he replied.

"So what?"

He dispatched a crew to free the woman's car.

Clogged sewer. Fallen power line. Crazed gas meter. Pickup swallowed by collapsed sinkhole. Deer crashed through the living room window, now eating potted orchids. Each ring brought news of the city's disarray.

Returning to the phone book, Gordon called for information about rheumatism, socialism, astral travel, and how to grow waterlilies in your bathtub. The trouble with dialing recorded messages, however, was that he had no chance to speak. Why should the owner of a cute voice remain mum? Although he had never flown anywhere, except back and forth between naval bases during his days in the Seabees, he called the airlines and inquired about fares and schedules to the far corners of the globe. He dialed the twenty-four-hour numbers of mutual funds to ask about investing money he didn't have. He discussed birth control options with Small Earth Inc., even though Mabel had long since made all the choices irrelevant. Brusque, efficient, the agents replied to his questions without saying a word about his voice.

So he dialed his own house. After quite a few rings, Mabel answered. At least the voice was a convincing imitation of her. "Honey," he said. "It's me."

"At four in the morning I don't care if it's God," she said. "I climbed up here to the kitchen imagining all kinds of disasters."

"Well, what do you think?" he murmured in his deepest baritone.

"About what?"

"About me using the phone."

"Good for you. Next you can master the washing machine."

"What do you mean? I keep fixing it, don't I?"

"I'm not talking repairs. I'm talking laundry."

"Okay, okay. So anyway, how do I sound?"

"Like always. Only smaller. Phones do that to everybody."

"Well, see you," said Gordon. "Kiss the kids for me. You got any messages you want me to write down?"

Midway through his question, Mabel clunked the receiver into its cradle. Gordon also hung up, but kept his hand on the sleek black phone, undecided whether to make a call or wait for one, sensing that the fate of the city depended on his lips and ears and itching fingers.

Weight

*G*ordon knew from experience that everything on Earth is doomed to sag. Roof beams, floor joists, the spines of horses, the stems of cut flowers, the heaps of dirt over graves, his wife's breasts, his own belly—minute by minute, all were yielding under the insistence of gravity. If he could believe the scientists on TV, even the planet was slowly shrinking from the pull of molten iron at its core.

Well-fed on Mabel's cooking, Gordon wasn't shrinking, but his abundant flesh was drooping on his bones. His jowls wobbled beneath his beard. The muscles of his arms and shoulders, still powerful enough to lift a couch, turned as soft as bread dough when they relaxed. His chest was slipping toward his waist, and his waist was slipping toward his butt, providing more territory for Mabel to clutch when they were making weary love.

"Pull a hunk of that loose," he told her one night as she squeezed him, "and I'll use it to make a tire for the truck."

"Then how would I find you in the dark?" said Mabel.

Never having outgrown the smushed homeliness of a newborn—homeliness remarked by everyone present at the birth, including his mother—Gordon didn't need to worry about losing his good looks.

What scared him was the prospect of losing his strength. Weekdays, he drove trucks or fixed them, welded girders, dug sewers, patched roads. Evenings and weekends he worked odd jobs, moving furniture, cleaning gutters, building fences, trimming trees, hauling trash. If he took a weekend off, the bill collectors started breathing down his neck because money leaked out of the checking account as fast as it trickled in. So if his body quit, the whole family would be in trouble.

There were enough people in his mortgaged house to field a softball team. At least for another fifteen years, until his mother and Mabel's parents (bless their souls) passed on, and the youngest of the kids finished college, and his checks began arriving from social security, he would have to carry the household on his back. This weighvt, more than his mashed face or thick legs, made him recall a tortoise he had seen at a backroads zoo when he was a boy. As he watched the ancient creature lumber slowly forward, three kids climbed onto its back, weighing the tortoise down until its belly scraped the ground, but still the scaly legs kept rowing.

The tortoise ambled into Gordon's thoughts one morning as he trimmed his beard at the basement sink. He was mulling over the electric bill, a clogged drain, a clattering tappet in the truck, Veronica's inflamed wisdom tooth, Papaw Hawkins's heart medicine. Gordon felt as though he was lugging bags of mortar, but the only bag visible in the mirror was his sagging paunch. He wasn't comforted to know that even the mirror glass, that slow liquid, was oozing downward, growing thicker at the bottom and thinner at the top—another factoid from the realm of science reported by Bruce.

When Mabel came in to brush her teeth and caught Gordon sucking in his gut, she said, "Too bad it comes right back as soon as you breathe."

Gordon let out a wheeze. "I wondered how I'd look with less belly."

"You'd look scrawny, and there'd be less of you to hug, and my mother would scold me for starving you." Mabel patted him on the rump. "Remember, I didn't marry you for your looks. I married you for your money."

"Right. Rich guys always have bedrooms in the basement and holes in their underwear."

"Show me one hole."

Gordon poked a finger through the seat of his boxer shorts.

"So why don't you put them in the mending?" Mabel said with a huff. "Am I supposed to keep track of everything?"

"Didn't the preacher say that at our wedding? Wife keeps track of everything?"

"If you really want to know," Mabel added, "it wasn't your money I fell in love with; it was your laugh."

Naturally, Gordon burst out with a laugh that shook the shower stall. He felt suddenly lighter. But then he noticed on the towel bar one of Mabel's bras, a garment both alluring and sad, the straps beginning to fray, the lacy cups stretched out of shape, and on his way to the bedroom he banged his toe against the jack post that shored up the kitchen floor, and he spied through the basement window the backyard cherry tree propped up by a two-by-four, and these reminders once more weighed him down.

That evening, after eight hours of overhauling the engine on a backhoe, Gordon perked up his ears when the grandparents returned from a meeting at the Golden Years Club to announce that they had joined the Society Against Gravity.

"It's called SAG for short," explained Papaw Hawkins, a man who had picked up a penchant for acronyms, as well as an ulcer, from his army days.

"Membership doesn't cost much at all," said Granny Mills. Tiny, dressed as usual in snazzy clothes she had bought dirt cheap at Goodwill, she knew the value of a dollar.

Gordon's mother-in-law, Mamaw Hawkins, a woman whose equatorial swelling and pockmarked skin made onlookers think of astronomy, declared that she had always suspected there was a cure for old age, and here at last it was.

The three grandparents were pushing eighty. Or eighty was pushing them. They had their foggy days, but mostly their minds were clear. They forgot names and sometimes lost their anchor in history, drifting about over the decades, confusing great nieces with long-vanished aunts, mixing up wars and presidents, yet sooner or later they remembered what needed remembering. They could sing all the verses from 1950s and '60s pop songs, they could work the crossword puzzles in the newspaper, and they could talk your arm and leg off about anything from politics to potatoes. But all three had grit in their joints that made them wince and fluttering in their organs that made them fret. They were slowing down. Mamaw and Papaw Hawkins were about half again as big as the doctor wanted them to be, while Gordon's wispy mother looked as though a three-cell flashlight would shine right through her.

"This better not be one of those cockamamie diets," Mabel warned. "If you think I'm cooking weird stuff, you've got another think coming."

Papaw Hawkins would eat anything that wouldn't eat him first, as he liked to say. On the other hand, the two grandmothers, who collected tips on health from TV and magazines, had always been persnickety about food. For weeks they had eaten nothing except tuna fish and grapefruit. This was followed by spells devoted to cucumbers, buttermilk, figs, and the dark meat of turkeys. No matter what the two old women put in their mouths, Mamaw Hawkins turned her meals into fat and Granny Mills turned hers into vapor. Sick and tired of catering to their food crazes, Mabel was glad to hear that the Society Against Gravity did not propose any bizarre diets.

"The point of SAG," Papaw Hawkins explained, "is not merely to reduce one's weight on the scales, but to defeat gravity altogether."

"How do you figure on doing that?" Gordon asked.

"Mind over matter," his mother answered, tapping her forehead with a bluish finger. Her circulation had always been poor; there was so little room in her for arteries and veins. As her skin turned transparent with age, she was taking on the color of watery sky.

"Meditation and machines," Mamaw Hawkins added.

They learned how to meditate by studying videos that arrived in the mail. Night after night, Gordon would trudge home from the city garage, where he wrestled with machines as old as dinosaurs, to find the grandparents squatting before the tube and staring at the image of a lotus blossom or candle flame, their faces screwed up in an effort to relax. They wore purple sweatshirts because that was the color of spirit, which weighed nothing. Bushed, Gordon would take off his boots and tiptoe past the old-timers to stir up the kids, who always retreated from these antics into various corners of the house; then he shuffled through the kitchen to hug Mabel, who rolled her eyes; and then he slouched down into the basement for his shower.

Membership in the Society Against Gravity brought the grandparents a monthly newsletter called *Lite*, posters of seagulls and astronauts, bumper stickers emblazoned with the word FLOAT, and an 800 number they could dial twenty-four hours a day for uplifting advice.

One Saturday morning a deliveryman staggered to the house lugging three large boxes that were stamped FRAGILE and ASSEMBLY REQUIRED. Each package held a device guaranteed to defy gravity, ordered by the grandparents from the back pages of the SAG newsletter. To cover all the angles, they had purchased three different models. One of these, meant to be worn around the waist, resembled a plump green doughnut.

Another was a jumbo backpack fitted with air jets. The third looked like a motorcycle helmet, with antennas sprouting from the top and a video screen in place of the visor, the whole apparatus as black and shiny as used crankcase oil. All three models were encrusted with enough dials and knobs to fill the cockpit of an airplane. That Saturday, Gordon and his father-in-law stayed up until midnight putting the gizmos together.

Next morning after church, where the minister preached about alternatives to heaven, the grandparents tested their gravity-defying machines. The backpack, whooshing and burping, lifted their heels from the linoleum. The helmet surrounded them with images of clouds that were so plausible the grandparents could have sworn they were floating. And the doughnut shook their bones with vibrations that might easily have been mistaken for weightlessness. Papaw Hawkins volunteered to wear all three devices at once, prompting Mamaw Hawkins to caution him about straining his cranky heart. But with the resolve of a veteran who had cruised in gunboats along the murky rivers of South Vietnam, dodging bullets, he forged ahead. Instead of releasing him from the bonds of Earth, however, the combination of helmet and backpack and doughnut merely befuddled him into laughter. Hearing the old man laugh, Gordon was reminded of how Mabel had acquired her taste for men who snort and roar.

"It's worse than tickling," said Papaw Hawkins when he had recovered his breath.

Mamaw Hawkins insisted that he sit down to recuperate.

Mabel arched an eyebrow at the whole business. She doubted the merits of anything ordered from the back pages of magazines, and she was mortally certain that neither meditation nor electronics could release one from the flesh. "Act your age," she told her father.

"But don't you see, dear," her mother said, "our age is what we're trying to outfox."

The four Mills children, expecting parents and grandparents to do freaky things, were no more embarrassed than usual by this latest fad.

The nearest any of them came to voicing a complaint was when Veronica, unable in adolescence to imagine ever growing old, said to Gordon, "I can't bring any of my friends home until the grands get over this hate-gravity thing."

Gordon looked at his daughter, whose downy skin and swaying walk had begun to fill the boys at school with dreams of flight. "They'll get over it soon enough," he said.

"Then what's next? Ouija boards? Bagpipes?" Disgusted with all grownups, Veronica sashayed toward the kitchen, where she would dial her friends from the wall phone, pretending it was the latest model of the classiest mobile.

As for Gordon, that Sunday he stayed up late pretending to read the newspaper until the rest of the family had gone to bed, and then in the darkened living room, while a video of fireflies played soundlessly on the television, he tried each of the gadgets in turn. Wearing the helmet, he could see nothing but sky and clouds, as if he were up high wheeling among the crows, but his feet never left the floor. The doughnut was a tight fit around his middle, and instead of making him feel weightless, it gave him the clammy sensation of a wet bathing suit. Before the backpack could lift him, the hiss of the air jets awakened Mabel, who came up the basement stairs in her nightgown and peered at him from beneath graying bangs that were turbulent from dreams.

"Gordon Ray Mills," she muttered, "after a quarter century of marriage, you still amaze me."

He shrugged free of the backpack and switched off the video. "I'm just checking out these contraptions to make sure they're safe."

"Give it up, you big oaf, and come to bed."

Gordon let his shoulders slump. He felt as though all the bags of cement, bundles of shingles, and stacks of lumber he had ever carried were piled on his shoulders. If he stood with his back to the kitchen door, where all the family heights were marked, would he still measure five feet nine? "Time to trade me in for a new model," he said.

"No, sir," Mabel shot back. "I worked too long training the old one. I'll stick with what I've got." She gripped him tenderly by the meat of his arm. "You'll feel better in the morning. So come."

The shampooed smell of her graying hair and the weariness in her eyes drew him to kiss her and then to follow her downstairs. By the time he settled beside her into his trough in the swaybacked mattress, Mabel was already twitching from sleep. He laid one of his callused hands on her thigh, gently, so as not to disturb her.

For Gordon, sleep seemed less like a drifting off than like a plunge into the abyss. Some nights, fear kept him from jumping. In falling you lost all sense of weight, as he knew from talking with buddies who had tumbled off ladders or scaffolds, but what you lost in awareness of gravity you made up for in terror. Tonight, while his body begged for rest, his mind clung to the world. He thought of his job, where he would have to report in a few hours and tackle all the breakdowns from the weekend. He ran through a long list of repairs that were needed on his own place. Even the antigravity gizmos, he realized, would eventually spring leaks and short out. He listened to the gas burner on the water heater kick in, hiss through a cycle, then kick off. The floor joists cricked as the wood lost the day's warmth. Mice skittered overhead through the heating ducts. Better clean that pilot light, Gordon thought, better check for termites, better set out mousetraps and bait them with peanut butter. Lying there, he felt heavier than ever, as though not only his own bulk but also the sleeping children and grandparents, the furniture, the ailing appliances, the drawers full of mortgage notes and insurance policies, the rusting van in the garage, the rattly pickup in the driveway, the attic stuffed with photographs and canceled checks and shabby suitcases, the entire aging house weighed down on him.

Turtles must sleep on their stomachs, he figured. If they got stuck upside down they would die. He rolled onto his belly and promptly dove into a dream in which he was his usual beefy self, except that a tortoise shell covered his back and he felt lighter than dandelion fluff.

He was swimming through the air above his neighborhood. No one looked up to see him, not the children playing catch on the sidewalk nor the drivers parked at the curb nor the garbage men banging cans, not even Mabel who was in the backyard hanging out clothes. Gordon parted his lips to call them but could make no sound. Although it was a brilliant day, he cast no shadow. The world had no smell. The wind passed through him without causing a tingle. Rowing along through the air, unburdened, he began to weep.

He woke to find himself not on his belly but on his back, with Mabel atop him. It was a measure of their fatigue that both had slept through the preliminaries of love, and now they were rocking toward the shore of an island they had reached together many times before and yet one they rediscovered each time as though it had just that moment risen from the sea.

Because tears in Gordon's eyes sparkled in the green light from the clock radio, Mabel whispered, "What's the matter, love? Did your back go out again? Am I too heavy?"

"No, no," he breathed, "you're light as a feather, and so am I."

The load of house and job and flesh would soon come pressing down again, but for an instant these foolhardy words held their own against the whine of bending metal and the yielding groans of wood.

Dance

When his back wasn't paining him, Gordon earned a few extra dollars on weekends by hauling furniture around the city in his pickup. Dented, rusty, equipped with heavy-duty shock absorbers and hydraulic tailgate lift, the truck bore on its flanks a painted sign:

MILLS THE MOVER—NO JOB TOO SMALL

Without need of a sign, Gordon's physique proclaimed him to be a lifter and carrier of heavy weights. Short, burly, with hands the size of hubcaps, pistons for legs, and a chest like a billboard for tattoos, he inspired, in those who bothered to glance at him, visions of twilit caves.

Customers who dialed the number painted on his truck rarely spoke with Gordon, who shied away from the phone, but they could leave a message with his wife, his children, his mother, or his parents-in-law. Yes, the family promised the callers, Gordon Mills would cheerfully move anything he could squeeze into his pickup. Couches or antique cupboards, mattresses or washing machines—it was all the same to him.

So it was that Gordon found himself early one Saturday hauling an upright piano from a music store to the Limestone Ballet Academy.

Gordon had invited his two younger kids to tag along, but they refused to unplug from TV cartoons; the older kids, up late gallivanting the night before, were still in bed; the wakeful grandparents were playing cards; and Mabel, who kept the house afloat, wouldn't dream of abandoning her post on a Saturday.

So Gordon drove alone to Malcolm's Music Emporium, where he loaded the piano onto his pickup. The black wooden case was mounted on casters, and a lucky thing, too: Gordon could lift a refrigerator, but this piano was heavier than a fridge. He lashed the piano down with ropes and then plowed through morning traffic toward the ballet studio. He could remember when the building that housed the ballet used to be a wholesale flower warehouse, and merchants from across the city and surrounding counties would congregate there before dawn to load their vans with carnations and gardenias and roses. The dancers must have occupied the warehouse for ten years or more, because when Jeanne, now in college, was a little girl, she had begged him to send her there for dancing lessons. Gordon had told her no, since the neighborhood of the school was too rough for her to ride there on the bus, and nobody else could spare the time to drive her so far. However, the truth was that the Mills household barely scraped by on Gordon's wages from the city, and lessons of any sort, whether in dance or music or art, had never fit in the budget.

Driving across the city with the piano gleaming like an oily engine block in his rearview mirror, Gordon wondered if, given those unaffordable lessons, Jeanne might have become a ballerina instead of a burger flipper working her way through college; he wondered if Bruce, making dough at a pizza joint after school, might have played the violin instead of video games; he wondered if Veronica, teetering on the edge of adolescence, might have dazzled the world in gymnastics. For Danny, just seven, crazy about drawing, there might still be hope—hope, but not a nickel more for lessons.

At the ballet school, Gordon backed up to the loading dock where tides of flowers used to flow in and out every day. This morning, amid the bottles and cigarette butts left there by winos, the dock held only a giant swan on wheels, an enormous angel with hinged wings, and a huge painting of a brick wall that leaned against the actual brick wall of the old warehouse. The world is filled with no end of odd things, Gordon thought as he lowered the tailgate, untied the ropes, and shoved the piano onto the platform.

Just then a tiny woman came bustling out. Dressed in black from head to foot, with a skirt that barely covered her rump and a hairdo like a rolled-up newspaper, she might have been a schoolgirl, except for a face that looked, despite a thick layer of makeup, as eroded as a vacant lot. "At last, at last, the piano man!" she cried. "Follow me."

This was easier said than done, for the woman darted through the hallways like a rabbit dodging a fox, while Gordon, a stranger here, plodded behind shoving the piano. She kept dashing around corners, disappearing from sight, and he kept making wrong turns, one of which led him to the doorway of a room where seamstresses hunched over their needles, foamy pink costumes billowing across their laps, and another led him to a room filled with old stage sets—balconies, stairways, towers, thrones—all jumbled together like the ruins of a collapsed city.

Maneuvering through the corridors, not daring to take his eyes off the piano, Gordon was vaguely aware of passing other tiny figures, more like children than grown-ups, really, more like elves than children. They were perched on benches and sprawled on the floor, dressing themselves in bright scraps of clothing that might have been torn from the backs of clowns. As the woman in black swept by, they bobbed their heads and murmured, "Madame, Madame."

When at last he ground to a halt, uncertain where to go next, the woman came charging back, lifted the violet eyeglasses that dangled from a chain about her neck, glared at him through the lenses, and commanded, "This way, this way! What's keeping you? The dancers are waiting!"

In fact, aside from a few pigeons roosting on the rafters, the only creature waiting in the ballet studio was the pianist, a weedy guy who clutched a bundle of sheet music and displayed, through an electric grin, a mouthful of teeth.

"Where do you want it?" Gordon asked the pianist.

"It isn't his business to want things," said the woman in black. "Just put it here," she added, skipping to one corner of the studio. Gordon trundled the piano after her, but no sooner had he reached the designated spot than the woman skipped back across the room, singing out, "No, no, better over here." They crisscrossed the room in this manner several times, Gordon following the woman and the pianist following Gordon, before the piano came to rest in the corner formed by a wall of mirrors and a wall of floor-to-ceiling windows.

"Leave it there for now," the woman said. "This is only a trial run, anyway, because we've never had much satisfaction from these upright models. Give me baby grands, I tell the board. But do they listen? Of course not. All the accountants think of is money, money, money! Uprights are cheap, they say. Grands are expensive. It's left to me to uphold the claims of art!"

Gordon straightened up, his backbone crackling. "While we're on the subject of money," he began, working himself to that awkward moment of asking for his pay.

The woman cut him off: "I expect I'll be sending the instrument right back to the store, so you must wait until the class is over."

"How long do you figure that'll be, ma'am?"

"Two hours. Three. What does it matter?"

This lady was one of those who gave commands as if she were ordering milkshakes and french fries through a loudspeaker at a drive-up window. Gordon could either kiss his wages goodbye and lift the hinged top of the piano and stuff her inside, or else pretend he was deaf to the sneer in her voice. Long practice and short cash had taught him to feign deafness. "Okay, then, ma'am," he said, "where do you want me to wait?"

"Anywhere! Anywhere! Just get out of my way!"

As he was turning to go, thinking he might walk the streets for a couple of hours, the pianist began playing, and in through the door streamed the dancers, the tiny elfin figures whom Gordon had seen dressing themselves in the bright colors of clowns. Snared by the music and by the troop of whirling, stretching, gesticulating figures, he backed into the far corner, away from the piano, the door, and the mirrors, lowered himself onto a folding chair, and hunkered down in an effort to become invisible. He might as well have been invisible, for all the notice anybody took of him.

The class began. The fingers of the pianist stormed over the keys, the teacher clapped time and barked orders, the dancers hooked their heels and fingers over wooden railings along the walls. Several times, to please his daughters, Gordon had watched ballet on television. On the screen, in costumes and makeup, the women looked like china dolls, the men like gods, and their movements defied the laws of gravity. Here in the studio, dressed in rags, without paint on their faces, grunting and panting, they struck him as miniature athletes. And yet, even while muffled in sweat suits, baggy socks, ripped T-shirts, and shawls, their bodies looked impossibly airy and limber. As they heated up and stripped off layers of clothing, Gordon wondered if, like onions, they might be peeled away to nothing. But at last the spindly arms and legs emerged, the backbones like strings of beads, the necks like the stems of flowers, and for the first time, he realized that all the dancers were female. Whether they were girls of ten or women of thirty, he couldn't have said, for without hips or breasts to speak of, hair tied up in knots, faces unmarked, they might have been any age.

For such a tiny woman, the teacher owned a large voice, which she boomed at the dancers. The pianist played as though his life depended on it—as though the more keys he struck per second, the more seconds he would be permitted to live. The dancers leaped and spun and twisted, seeming to float in midair, balancing on their pointed shoes. Watching them, Gordon thought of birds, kites, windblown leaves. Watching them, he forgot himself, forgot his thick bones and heavy flesh, forgot his stiffening joints, forgot he was a troll visiting the empire of elves.

All unawares, Gordon stood up from the chair, shuffled his clumsy feet in time with the music, took a little skip, and then, surprised by the softness of his landing, jumped higher, still higher, and then he rose, legs treading the air. In the wall of mirrors, he could see his grinning, bearded, pumpkin-shaped head rise above the tribe of ballerinas, drift up between the fluorescent lights, and float among the rafters. Until the teacher clapped her hands and the piano fell silent and the dancers yielded to the rule of gravity, Gordon could hover there in that weightless moment, seized by grace, high among the rafters in a whirl of pigeon feathers and the scintillating dust of flowers.

Crows

Once, as a boy, Gordon fired his BB gun at a crow, not because he had any grudges against crows but because he had just watched a movie about Davy Crockett, who could shoot the whiskers off a squirrel from a hundred yards away with a muzzle-loading rifle. Gordon's aim wasn't so sharp. Instead of squawking from the sting of a BB, the crow glared at him, flew to a branch directly above his head, and loosed a stream of white slime.

News of that errant shot must have been passed down from one generation of birds to the next because decades later, every crow in the neighborhood still scolded Gordon. They would cock their heads and croak at him, drop sticks on him, or waddle up and untie the laces on his boots. If he left his lunch pail uncovered, they would sneak up and steal a sandwich. Once, they put roofing nails on the driveway to puncture the tires on his truck. They mimicked his laugh, which his children compared to a coyote's howl, and they slouched along in imitation of his walk, which his children compared to the rolling gait of a gorilla.

It was bad enough being mocked by his kids without also being mocked by birds. Chickadees or sparrows or goldfinches would have been easier to ignore, for they were small and shy, with chirpy voices. But crows were big and loud, as brash as schoolyard bullies. Although

Gordon was by nature a peaceful man, back when he still spent recess time in schoolyards, he dealt with bullies by thrashing them. But he couldn't thrash crows. In their beady eyes, he supposed, *he* was the bully, for having shot that ill-aimed BB at one of their clan long ago.

"It's bad karma," explained Gordon's older son, Bruce, who, at sixteen, had become all-knowing. Bruce had likewise come to realize the full extent of his father's ignorance. So he patiently defined bad karma as the legacy of your past mischief, like the buildup of tartar on your teeth or cholesterol in your veins. Fortunately, he added, there were ways of undoing the damage.

"Give me a for-instance," Gordon muttered as he pulled off his grimy overalls after a day at the city maintenance garage.

Bruce couldn't very well urge his father to quit work and go meditate in a cave, for that would wreck the family finances, and he had too much affection for the old man to suggest an early death followed by reincarnation as a wiser being. So he advised: "You could do the crows a good turn, which might persuade them to forgive you."

It so happened that the city of Limestone, Indiana, little known to the rest of the world, had recently become well known among crows, which flocked there in the fall and settled in for the winter, roosting by the thousands on trees and rooftops. Branches snapped and power lines sagged under their weight. Gordon couldn't go anywhere without setting off a flurry of cackles and caws. Black eyes, gleaming with suspicion, followed his every move. He took to wearing a hard hat whenever he went outside to protect himself from their droppings.

At least he was no longer the only one afflicted, as the siege of crows darkened the sky and whitened everything beneath their roosts. A slippery icing coated sidewalks, war memorials, fire hydrants, and street signs. People who ventured out, clad in slickers with the hoods pulled

up, often got lost, as after a blizzard. School was delayed each morning until the streets could be flushed to keep the buses from skidding.
The crows plucked letters from mailboxes and newspapers from front
lawns, leaving behind a trail of confetti. They rang doorbells in the wee
hours, spooked toddlers, harassed dogs, waltzed into cafés to peck at
plates, raided garbage cans, and took over the dumpsters from rats.

A task force appointed by the mayor to repel the invasion naturally
began by recommending that scarecrows be erected throughout the city.
No sooner were the scarecrows in place, dressed in castoff clothes, than
the birds perched atop the straw-stuffed heads and wooden arms, blithely preening. Undaunted, the task force tried more strenuous remedies.
Broadcasting crow distress calls merely elicited yawns from the real crows.
Playing rock and roll at top volume beneath their roosts only inspired them
to dance. Feisty cats sent to spook them soon retreated, much the worse
for wear, often missing an ear or a tail. When heaps of old tires were set on
fire to smoke them out, the crows moved to the roofs of houses, where they
chattered all night, keeping the inhabitants awake. An assault by fireworks
provoked the birds to drop gravel onto parked cars, especially on sport
utility vehicles, which presented the largest targets.

"You see why it's called a murder of crows," Bruce remarked to his
father, who of course didn't have a clue. With a sigh, Bruce explained
that just as a bunch of cows is a herd and a bunch of fish is a school, so
a gang of crows is a murder.

"Who thought that one up?" Gordon asked.

This further evidence of his father's ignorance prompted another
sigh from Bruce, who declared that God had thought up the expression,
which appeared in the Bible. Not actually having read the Bible, and
uncertain of his facts, Bruce moved on, hastening to lay out a scheme
that would simultaneously free the city from the plague of crows and
free his father from their curse.

Gordon agreed to give the plan a try. So on his next day off work, he
and Bruce drove to Stone Country Brewery, where they loaded the bed

of the pickup with a stinking heap of spent barley and hops. Next they drove to the courthouse square, where the oaks and maples were clotted with crows. Bruce got out, climbed in back, and dumped a shovelful of brewery waste onto the ground. Half a dozen crows immediately flew down to investigate, pecking here and there, blinking in apparent bliss, and then they chuckled enthusiastically, whereupon fifty or a hundred other crows swooped down from the trees to join them.

Following the plan, Gordon rolled the truck slowly out of town along the road leading to the dump, while Bruce kept shoveling fermented grain over the tailgate. Crows followed them in an ever-swelling flock, strutting and then waddling and finally staggering from one pungent pile to the next. By the time the procession reached the dump, those crows still capable of flying were doing loop-the-loops. Some crows dangled upside down from telephone wires, clinging by their feet; others picked up trash in their beaks and flung it in the air; and still others sprawled on the rubbish, out cold.

Bruce scattered the last of the mash and then knocked on the rear window, the signal for Gordon to show himself. Bracing for an onslaught of jeers, Gordon climbed from the truck and was surprised to hear the multitude of crows chortling contentedly. Two birds even fluttered up and perched on his shoulders, one on each side, babbling with gratitude and rubbing their feathery jowls against his chin. Then they leaped down, wobbled a few steps, and flopped onto their bellies for a snooze. Dopey murmurs arose from near and far. The few crows still awake were inspecting the garbage, muttering their approval over half-eaten pizzas, soggy french fries, rancid hotdogs, and other tasty morsels.

To assure that the birds would stay at the landfill, Gordon and Bruce cruised the highways near the city, scraping up roadkill, until the truck was heaped high with mangled deer and flattened raccoons and unlucky possums. They unloaded their haul back at the dump, where feathered lumps were beginning to stir. As the crows awoke to discover this offering of carcasses, which stank to high heaven, they clacked their bills in a way that sounded very much like applause.

Rabbit

Only the first three of the Mills children had been planned, as much as the calamitous arrival of children could ever be planned. The fourth child, Danny, was what the Cajun mechanic at the city garage called a lagniappe—an extra, a sweet present you had no reason to expect, like the baker's gift of a thirteenth donut when you paid for a dozen.

"He was a mistake," Mabel admitted to friends when Danny was out of earshot, "but the best one I ever made."

Danny was a favorite of the elderly couple who lived next door, Ella and Ray, whose last name had as many letters as the alphabet and syllables that zigzagged in baffling directions, which is why they invited all the neighbors, including children, to call them simply Ella and Ray. Danny knew they were old, even older than his grandparents, who were ancient, so one day when he came home from first grade and saw Ella and Ray out back of their house sipping iced tea on their patio, he went over to ask if they had sailed on the ark with Noah and the dinosaurs. Ray drew his wrinkled face into a smile and answered, "No, pumpkin, we missed the boat."

"Then how'd you get through the flood?"

"We hitched a ride on a hippo, who kept swimming until the rain let up and a mountain appeared, and Ella and I stepped back onto dry land."

This account satisfied Danny, who shared the information with the rest of the Mills household at supper.

Living next door to the Mills clan would have tried the patience of saints while Danny and the three older kids were growing up. Without children of their own, Ray and Ella seemed to enjoy the tumult. At least they never complained about the firecrackers, caterwauling, skateboard screeching, midnight shenanigans, and other disruptions from the boisterous kids. Even the occasional broken window from an errant baseball didn't faze Ray and Ella because Gordon always replaced the glass the next day.

By the time Danny asked his question about Noah's ark, Ray and Ella must have been well north of eighty, Gordon figured, a decade older than his own mother, and he could see they were beginning to fail. So Gordon kept an eye on Ray, making sure the old man didn't climb a ladder or run a chainsaw or do anything else endangering life and limb. Once or twice a week, Mabel dropped by to chat with Ella, usually taking a casserole, a bouquet of cut flowers from the yard, or some other small gift. The Mills children ran errands for the old couple, returning library books or picking up groceries. Even Danny found chores to do, such as rearranging their patio furniture or digging holes in their lawn where they might want to plant trees someday.

One Saturday morning, Gordon noticed a crate the size of a phone booth resting on Ray and Ella's front walk. The old man was out there prying at the wood with a crowbar, grunting and groaning, without making any headway. Gordon hurried over to lend a hand. Ray surrendered the crowbar and then limped away into the garage. Moments later he returned, dragging a green tarp. "Here," he said, "throw this over the top so Ella won't see. It's for her birthday tomorrow."

Gordon finished dismantling the crate under cover of the tarp, eventually revealing a concrete rabbit tall enough to look him in the eye.

The rabbit's eyes were painted blue, and the fur was pink. It stood upright on its hind legs, balancing a tray on one lifted forepaw like a waiter delivering a drink, an impression reinforced by the fact that it was wearing a red jacket and shiny black leather shoes. The pointy ears stood straight up, as if electrified.

Ray ducked under the tarp to admire the statue alongside Gordon. "Found it in Chicago," the old man said. "You need first-rate art, you go to Chicago."

"Was Ella wanting a concrete rabbit?" Gordon asked.

"She wanted a live one, but I'm allergic to fur. So I figured this was the next best thing." Ray set a folded note on the rabbit's tray and weighted it down with a stone. "Come over tomorrow morning to see Ella's face when I unveil this beauty."

Next morning, the nine members of the Mills household were eating pancakes when they noticed Ray and Ella shuffling out toward the green bundle, so they all trooped over, the children still in pajamas, to watch the unveiling. When the giant rabbit emerged, Ella gave a gasp of surprise, hugged Ray, and started bawling.

Danny sidled over to grasp her hand, saying, "Don't cry, Ella."

"I'm just flabbergasted," she sobbed.

By standing on tiptoes, Danny could peek over the lip of the rabbit's tray. He lifted the stone and handed the folded paper to Ella, who smiled through her tears when she read it.

The Mills never learned what that note said, but they learned about many later ones. Every night Ray left a folded paper on the rabbit's tray, and every morning Ella tottered out to retrieve it. Before Ella stirred, however, Danny would steal over there with a flashlight, decipher the message using his amazing new reading skills, and return home to recite it for the family. "You're the bee's knees," the note might say, or "I'm the fella for Ella," or "Sugar pie, I'm your guy." Every note was signed, "Forever, Ray."

Danny recalled that signature with puzzlement when Ray was hauled away in a hearse a few months after the concrete rabbit appeared. Mabel explained that Ray didn't mean he'd live forever, only that he'd never quit loving Ella. Danny wasn't sure what to think of love, which could make you laugh and cry at the same time, nor did he know how long death would last. As he waited for Ray to return, he noticed that now Ella was placing a note on the rabbit's tray each morning. Because she didn't lay a stone on top, the paper would flutter away on the wind. Every day, after returning from school, Danny scoured the neighborhood, finding notes in bushes, on the hoods of cars, in goldfish ponds. He found them woven into birds' nests, caught in bicycle spokes, flattened against fences, snared in porch railings, skittering along sidewalks. He memorized each message, sounding out the letters, and then he let the wind carry it on.

At supper he repeated Ella's words, which puzzled him as much as Ray's disappearance. "Dancing in the kitchen," a note might say, or "No kids but lots of kicks," or "Rag and bone shop of the heart," or "Meet you in harp city." As Danny recited the messages, he studied the faces of his brother and sisters, where he saw a bit of understanding, and he saw a bit more in the faces of his parents, and yet more in his grandparents. Evidently there were secrets hidden in those notes, secrets he might learn to read if he lived as long as Noah or even if he only lived as long as Ella and Ray.

Fossil

*I*f all the dirt that Gordon had ever dug was heaped in one place, along with all the sand and gravel he had shoveled and the stone he had moved and the firewood he had stacked, how big would that pile be? A lot bigger than his two-story house, he figured, bigger than the Unitarian Universalist church he attended when his tricky back allowed him to sit for an hour in a wooden chair, bigger even than the county jail, which was expanding faster than the population that supplied it with prisoners.

Gordon was musing on these points of comparison one morning while digging a trench for a new sewer line in the street out front of the jail. He was making good progress with the backhoe—a machine he maneuvered so deftly, his coworkers claimed, that he could make a kitten purr by stroking its belly with the bucket—when he noticed gray knobs of stone showing through the red clay at the bottom of the hole. Dad burn it, he thought. Needing to see whether he had run into rubble, which could easily be cleared, or bedrock, which couldn't, he climbed down from the backhoe, grabbed a shovel, and lowered himself into the trench, a move that gave him the willies. Then he scraped the clay aside, gradually uncovering those gray knobs, which proved to be the stony outcroppings of a businessman.

He would later be informed that what he had found embedded in the limestone ledge was not the businessman himself, but a fossil replica, minerals having seeped in to replace the flesh and clothes, thread by thread and cell by cell. Not yet wised up by the experts, however, when Gordon spied the wingtip shoes, creased trouser cuffs, and brim of a bowler hat, he shouted to his supervisor, "Hey, boss, we got us a guy in a suit buried down here! A banker, looks like, or maybe a lawyer!"

"If it's not one thing, it's another," the supervisor grumbled.

Whenever an excavation by the city maintenance crew turned up signs of earlier life—mammoth tusks, dinosaur bones, clay pots, old coins, charred wood, horseshoes, skeletons—the digging had to stop, and the supervisor had to notify the state archaeologist. Once you called in the scientists, you could kiss your work schedule goodbye. But regulations were regulations, so he telephoned Indianapolis, and a few days later officials showed up bearing cameras and survey equipment.

Gordon was glad to let the scientists take over the job of grubbing down in the trench. Put him on a backhoe, a bulldozer, or an earth-mover—machines he'd learned to use in the Seabees—and he felt at ease. So long as he could sit up high on a seat, with a diesel roaring beneath him, he would shift dirt and stone from dawn until dark. Or give him a jackhammer and he would break any size hole you wanted in concrete or blacktop, just so long as he could keep his feet planted on the ground. Bred for the open air, he felt stifled down in holes, which always seemed about to close in on him. One of the worst jobs he ever had was cleaning out the cave where centaurs and other beasts hung out for a while before moving on to parts unknown, and in the cave, at least, he had the company of those talkative critters to help him forget he was underground.

He rarely pondered where his feelings came from, imagining they just rose up and died away without rhyme or reason, wayward as the wind, but he did know the source of this particular feeling, this fear of being buried, because it had come over him suddenly at age sixteen, the day he learned that his father, a quarrier who mucked around for twenty years in one pit after another, was crushed under a ten-ton block of limestone. "Never would have happened if he'd been sober," Gordon's mother still insisted.

Never would have happened if he'd stayed out of that hole, Gordon thought.

In hopes of hurrying things along at the excavation, the supervisor assigned Gordon to help the archaeologists with any chores they needed him to do.

"I'd just as soon stay at the garage and keep busy," Gordon said.

"Don't you worry," said the supervisor. "They'll keep you hopping. I've never seen a white coat who didn't like to order folks around."

None of the scientists and technicians who showed up to examine the fossil actually wore a white coat. They were dressed, in fact, like farmers or loggers, even the women, in stained blue jeans and flannel shirts and leather work boots. One of them turned out to be the state archaeologist herself, a woman taller than Gordon and about twenty years younger, with broken fingernails and a voice like the sound of tires on gravel. No telling how many degrees from universities she had, this Dr. Jeffrey, but to look at her, you'd think she earned a living by laying bricks or milking cows. She was the brains and boss of this outfit, though, as Gordon could tell by the way the others leaned in close to catch her least word.

He could also tell, by the way Dr. Jeffrey hopped right down into the trench, that she had no fear of burial. She bent low to study the fossilized wingtip shoes, trouser cuffs, and bowler hat, measured here and there, then ordered her crew to saw out a block large enough to contain the specimen. Turning to Gordon, and looking him over quizzically, as though trying to place his squat frame and bearded mug on the evolutionary tree, she asked if he could build a crate for shipping the block across town to the college, where technicians would chisel the body free of its limestone jacket.

"Sure, I can build you a crate," Gordon answered.

"It has to be sturdy," she warned, "or the specimen will be damaged."

"I'll dovetail the joints if you want me to, ma'am."

"Nothing fancy, please. Just make sure it doesn't fall apart in transit."

Maybe this Dr. Jeffrey was too young, Gordon allowed, or maybe she had worked with too many slouches and slobs. If a guy needed to be *told* to do a good job, he'd never do a good job. Using Indiana red oak and carbon steel bolts, Gordon would build a crate strong enough to hold a tornado, let alone a stone businessman. Although a crack here and there wouldn't bother the old gent at this late date, long after he had settled into the ooze of an ancient sea, and although it might not bother the archaeologists, accustomed as they were to botched evidence, it would bother Gordon no end. From the moment he cut the first board and tightened the first bolt, his reputation as a craftsman was bound up with the fate of the fossil. He delivered the crate in two days.

Of course the diamond saws used to slice the bedrock might already have opened hairline fissures. For that matter, the businessman might have been damaged long before the sewer excavation revealed those wingtip shoes, his body shaken by earthquakes, fractured by freezes and thaws, dissolved by subterranean waters, or throttled by roots. It seemed unlikely that any fossil, especially one the size and shape of a businessman, could emerge from its burial without flaws. A few more cracks wouldn't be a big deal, Gordon thought. Nonetheless, as the block was loaded into the crate and the crate was hoisted from the trench, he watched anxiously as the crane operator feathered back on the winch, easing the stone onto the flatbed truck without a bump.

Gordon followed the flatbed to the college football stadium, where a temporary laboratory had been set up beneath the grandstands. Piece by piece, with wrenches and patience, he took the crate apart, while Dr. Jeffrey stood watching, arms crossed over her chest, eyes narrowed, as if waiting for him to fumble. Well, she'd have to wait a good long while. He loosened the last bolt and removed the last oak plank without a hitch. "There's your fossil, doctor, safe and sound," he said. "I hope you get him out in one piece."

"What leads you to say *him*?" the archaeologist asked.

Mabel, Jeanne, and Veronica had lectured Gordon on what they called gender stereotypes. So he tried again. "I hope you get *her* out in one piece," he said, although in truth he considered the shoes too big for a woman.

"*Her*?" Dr. Jeffrey repeated scornfully. What could legitimately be identified at this early point in the investigation, she went on to explain, was not properly speaking a "businessman" at all, far less a "business-woman," not even the fossil replica of one, but rather a slab of lime-stone containing shapes that looked remarkably like a hat brim, trouser cuffs, and a pair of well-shod feet. Laypeople might leap to conclusions, she told Gordon, but a scientist must withhold judgment until all the evidence has been gathered and carefully examined. These odd shapes might turn out to be nothing more than records of wave action in ancient seas or the whimsical contours of a fossilized coral reef.

On the evening after the uncrating of the specimen, Granny Mills went to a square dance at the Senior Center, but by a rare conjunction of orbits the other eight members of the household were gathered for supper: Gordon and Mabel, Mamaw and Papaw Hawkins, and the four children. They were enjoying Mabel's chili and baking powder biscuits while Gordon brought them up to date on the fossil. Between bites, Danny, the ever curious first-grader, asked him, "How does an ocean make rock?"

Gordon had asked the same question of the scientists, and he repeated what he could remember of their answer: "Sea creatures pull
chemicals out of the water to make their shells, and when they die the
shells sink to the bottom and pile up and get smushed and turn into
limestone."

"How do all those mushed-up shells stick together?"

"You stumped me there, kiddo," said Gordon, who felt that for every
square foot of new knowledge he gained, his ignorance expanded by
an acre.

"They're cemented together with calcium carbonate under the pressure of water," said Bruce, who rarely missed a chance to enlighten
his benighted family by offering facts gleaned from his omnivorous
reading.

"So how long has that dude been stuck there in the rock?" Danny
asked.

"A long time," Gordon answered. "Millions and millions of years,
they tell me."

"Poor thing must have died in the flood," Mamaw Hawkins suggested, a notion left over from her evangelical upbringing and not yet
erased by having switched her allegiance to the Unitarians, who believed in the gospel of science.

"Millions of years!" said Danny. "That makes him almost as old as
you, Pops."

"Pretty near," Gordon said.

"Daddy, tell us how you used to hunt woolly mammoths," put in
Veronica, the cheeky middle-schooler.

"Cut it out, you two," said Mabel. "Don't make your father feel old
before his time. Can't you see he's still a spring chicken?"

Danny poured honey on a biscuit and stuffed his mouth, enforcing
a pause in his questions, which allowed Gordon to recall the time ages
earlier when he had truly felt as fresh and cocky as a young rooster, way
back when his own father was still around for teasing. Nowadays, he

felt as though he was halfway to becoming a fossil himself, his arteries hardening, joints stiffening, bones turning brittle. If his father had been left buried in the limey ooze of that quarry, would the body have turned to stone? Would minerals have taken on the old man's shape, grain by grain, forming a dimple in the chin, a bulge for the whiskey belly, traces of scars on the hands, and veins on the bandy legs? Gordon blinked, longing to hear, amid the laughter and storytelling at the dinner table, the smoker's cough and raspy voice of his old man.

Once a week or so on his way home from the city garage, Gordon stopped by the football stadium to see how work on the fossil was coming along. Usually, there was only one technician in the lab, a scrawny young guy with pasty skin who looked like he hadn't seen the sun in quite a while. He sat hunched over the limestone slab, loosening grit with a tiny drill, then whisking the spot clean and examining the result through a magnifying lens. Then he loosened some more grit, brushed it away, and peered through the magnifying glass, repeating the process over and over. At the rate he was going, he might take as long to expose the fossil as the ocean took to make it.

From one visit to the next, Gordon could see hardly any progress. "Moving right along!" he would say, thinking to put a little oomph in the sluggish guy. The technician only glanced up briefly and scowled, his pale eyes seeming not to focus without benefit of the magnifying lens.

Occasionally, Gordon happened to be on the scene when the archaeologist and her team arrived to study the fossil. Dr. Jeffrey would not extend her surmises one inch beyond the point which the technician had most recently uncovered. "What we see here," she declared on one of her visits, lightly fingering the businessman's lower extremities, "might perhaps be characterized as shoe-oid or trouser-oid in form, but we must reserve judgment."

When Dr. Jeffrey's back was turned, however, the assistants, less rigorously trained, speculated on whether the trousers would be pleated or plain, the suit coat double-breasted or single, the tie narrow or wide. Would he wear a pin in his lapel? Would he wear glasses, and, if so, would they be horn-rimmed or wire-framed? They laid friendly bets on what style the coat would turn out to be—French-cut or Italian? three-button sleeves or two?—and on what expression the face would be found to wear—grim or nonchalant? discouraged or cocky? Throwing aside all professional cautions, the assistants envisioned in detail the entire businessman when only a portion had been exposed, and this reckless imagining would no doubt bar them from ever gaining tenure at the college or succeeding to the position of state archaeologist.

Meanwhile, Gordon kept an eye out for any sign of damage to the businessman. The fossil, as it slowly emerged from the stone, was in fact badly riven by cracks. Most of these appeared ancient, stained rusty red or inky black, the edges buffed by erosion. But some few looked fresh, like the cracks in eggs at the bottom of a grocery bag.

"Those cracks make him look like concrete that set up too quick," Gordon said to the pasty technician.

"I'm certainly not to blame," the young man insisted. "I work so carefully I couldn't possibly have injured the specimen. If you ask me, the crate wasn't suitable."

"What are you talking about? Why, that crate was stout enough to hold the pyramids of Egypt." Even as he uttered the words, Gordon realized he could have added more padding to keep the stone from jostling, could have used more cross braces to keep the crate from wracking, and he felt a flush of shame.

He avoided the laboratory for a month. On returning, he found that the technician had uncovered the businessman's knees, where the trouser creases were flattened as though from habitual crossing of the legs. The lower half of a tightly furled umbrella was exposed beside the knees on one side, and on the other side appeared the accordioned bottom of a briefcase. Dr. Jeffrey, stopping by with her assistants, and unwilling to admit that the briefcase was in fact a briefcase, spoke of using x-ray crystallography to determine whether it might, instead, be a petrified clam.

When, after some weeks of finicky grinding, the entire briefcase lay exposed, and the tails of the suit coat (flared over the businessman's ample rump) finally appeared, equipment was hauled in to shoot gamma rays through the stone in an effort to discover what papers he'd been carrying and what food he'd been digesting at the time of his demise. The briefcase was found to be crammed with legal papers, and the stomach with eggs and croissants and beer.

Still refusing to jump to conclusions, Dr. Jeffrey kept an open mind about these discoveries, but her assistants conjectured freely about the man's age, religion, position in the corporate flowchart, sex life, and psyche. It puzzled Gordon, when he stopped by on his way home from work, to hear them talking about the businessman's neuroses and phobias, his liminal states, and mythic archetypes. They might as well have been speaking Cherokee for all the sense he could make of their lingo. Whenever bookish talk went over his head, he felt a twinge of regret for having dropped out of high school to join the navy. But with his father dead from drink—or from limestone, depending on which version you believed—who else was going to support his mom?

In the coming weeks, Gordon felt more than a twinge of regret as a host of fractures appeared in the fossil businessman, fractures that might have been caused by any number of disturbances—meteor impacts, say, or underground nuclear tests, or continental drift—but they could just as well have been caused by flaws in the crate. He lay awake nights thinking of what he might have done wrong and hoping he would be given another chance to prove his skill.

Still brooding on the fractured fossil, Gordon was at his workbench in the garage one Saturday morning, deciding which of the many items on his list of household chores to tackle first, when Veronica slipped out from the kitchen, moving so quietly that he was startled when she said, "Daddy?"

He knew from the way she used her little-girl voice that she wanted to be sure he wouldn't say no to whatever she was about to ask him. "Hey, there, hon," he said, turning to smile at her. He noticed she was carrying one of her nature magazines. "What gets you out of bed so early on a weekend?"

"Well, I was wondering," she said, twirling a finger in her black ponytail, "if you're not too busy, could you make a little something for me?"

"Never too busy for you, kiddo. What are you wanting to make?"

"A bluebird house."

"Expecting bluebirds, are you?"

"They're due up here from the South any day now."

"Then we'd better get them a house ready."

Beaming, she opened the magazine to show him a photograph. "Here's what it should look like."

Gordon pushed aside his to-do list and spread the magazine on his workbench to study the photo. Veronica curled an arm around his waist and snuggled against him, as if she had forgotten for the moment that she was twelve years old. In no hurry for the moment to pass, he estimated the dimensions, calculated the materials they would need, and pictured every step in the project before he touched a tool.

Then the two of them set to work. Gordon ran the table saw, drill press, and sander, while Veronica specified every detail of the design.

Two hours later, the garage smelled of sawdust and the little pine house was finished, with a slanting roof, an entrance hole the precise diameter favored by bluebirds, every joint neatly fitted, every edge sanded smooth. One side of the box was hinged, so it could be opened "to check on the chicks," as Veronica said.

After another half hour, Gordon had mounted the birdhouse on a steel post in a spot in the yard surrounded by scruffy grass, with an aluminum baffle on the post to keep snakes from crawling up, and the front of the box facing east—all according to Veronica's directions, for she knew as much about bluebirds, Gordon reckoned, as he knew about bulldozers. She gave him a kiss on the cheek, another rarity at this stage in her life, and then she hurried inside to fetch her binoculars.

Gordon carried the tingle of that kiss back into the garage, where he found Mabel rooting around in his bin of scrap wood.

"What're you looking for, favorite wife of mine?" he asked.

"That chopping block I bought at a yard sale, thinking you could use it to make me a knife rack someday. Since you've got your tools out and sawdust all over the place, I thought maybe you could make it today."

"I bet I could," Gordon said.

He was at work on Mabel's knife rack when Jeanne, having heard the roar of the saw, came out to ask if he would make her a bookshelf next. Then Bruce requested a tripod for the telescope he'd bought with money he earned at the pizza joint. Granny Mills let Gordon know that a wooden stool would make it so much easier for her to climb up onto her four-poster bed. Mamaw Hawkins asked for a sturdy new quilting frame to replace her old rickety one and brought a diagram to show just the kind she wanted. Papaw Hawkins requested a rack to hold his tobacco pipes, which he kept around for the sake of their aroma, even though he had long since given up smoking at the insistence of the grandkids.

The last member of the family to put in a carpentry request was Danny, who burst into the garage late Sunday afternoon saying, "Pops, I know you can make anything, so I'm hoping you'll make a new home for my gerbils."

"What's wrong with their cage?" Gordon asked.

"It's boring."

"How do you know?"

"They told me."

"So what do you have in mind?"

"A castle," Danny said, holding up a sheet of paper. "See, I've got it all drawn out. There's a courtyard and towers and ladders going every which way, and a flagpole and maybe a dungeon, and a drawbridge and a moat for sure. You can do it, can't you, Pops?"

"I'll give it a shot," Gordon said, "but I'll need your help. So hang on to your picture, and we'll get started just as soon as I finish a few other jobs."

Danny gave a yip of delight and ran outside.

Gordon was adding *gerbil castle* to the list of projects when Veronica stole in quietly from the yard to announce that a male bluebird was perched atop the little pine house, singing away, while his mate was fetching grass and straw for the nest.

"Think we'll get some chicks?" Gordon asked.

"Oh, I hope so!" Veronica said, her dark eyes gleaming. She gave him a hug, whispered, "You're the best!" then ran back outside to watch the birds.

Trash

During his tours of duty on the garbage crew, Gordon enjoyed more than anything else the spell of stillness in the predawn city before he started his truck. Indoors at that hour, new parents walked their colicky babies, security guards watched flickering monitors, bakers kneaded yeasty dough, janitors mopped hallways, and lovers lay wrapped in one another's arms; but the outdoors belonged to trash collectors and cats. Even the city's homeless people, drifters during the day, were still curled about their wary dreams in church basements and city shelters, and cops in idling squad cars drowsed to the chatter of radios.

Gordon made a point of reaching the equipment yard before anyone else so he could sit in the cab of his truck, breathe in the syrupy smell of rotting food scraps, and feel the sleeping avenues drawn about him like a quilt. When he arrived, there was still no hint of sun, not even on the longest days of summer. Airplane beacons flashed on radio towers. Wind sang through power lines. The streetlamps did not so much illuminate the night as carve it up into zones of darkness. As his vision began to dim from cataracts, Gordon could no longer track the planets or see any except the brightest stars, but he could still watch the moon filling and emptying like a bowl of milk. Once in a great while, on mornings of absolute clarity, he spied the glittering flag of the Milky Way unfurled across the sky.

Eventually the supervisor trudged in, clipboard under his arm, then a few drivers and loaders, each wearing a vest with a Day-Glo orange *X* on front and back that marked them in the gloom like targets, and the spell was broken. Time to earn my keep, Gordon thought. He cranked the engine, which quickly smothered all other smells under the stink of diesel exhaust. When his own loader showed up—a teenager named Zeke, too young for this work, too scrawny, should have been in school—it was time to pull out.

There used to be two loaders for each truck, and drivers only drove. But in a recent campaign for reelection, the mayor decided in the middle of a speech to show the voters what a pinchpenny he was. "Why pay two men to load," he mused before the television cameras, "when there's a driver sitting up front with a strong back and a pair of hands? I say, let him get off his duff and pitch in!"

Gordon was burly, all right, and on good days he could still heft double his own weight, but he was no longer young, and over the years his back had grown finicky. "Before we try surgery," the doctor had told him, "let's give your back a rest to see if it can heal itself."

"How long a rest?" Gordon asked.

"Oh, six months at least," the doctor answered.

Knock off work for half a year? If he took that long a break, he'd lose his job for sure, and the family would end up eating at the community kitchen and sleeping in church basements.

The supervisor was just as intent on keeping his handiest employee as Gordon was intent on keeping his job. So whenever Gordon's back was acting up, the supervisor reassigned him from the usual heavy lifting on the city maintenance crew to some lighter duty, such as driving a garbage truck.

"Mills, you just sit up there in the cab like a king on his throne," said the supervisor, "and let the loaders do the hard work."

Now, however, thanks to the mayor's thrift, Gordon not only had to drive from house to house, but also at every stop he had to set the parking brake, turn on the flashers, climb down from the cab, join Zeke in dragging cans and bags and bundled limbs to the rear of the truck, and then hoist everything into the hopper, limp back to the cab, climb onto the seat, stomp the clutch, shove the gear into first, release the brake, turn off the flashers, and ease forward to the next stop—where it was all to do over again.

Still, there were compensations. Folks tossed out fixable things—a lawn chair with a torn seat, a bicycle with a bent wheel, a toaster that wouldn't heat, a leaf blower that wouldn't start, a birdcage lacking a door, a basketball with a leak, a vacuum cleaner missing a power cord, and enough other stuff to fill Gordon's garage. On weekends when he wasn't working odd jobs, he repaired the discards and then gave the mended items to neighbors or donated them to Goodwill or added them to his cluttered household.

In winter, when his gloves froze to the handles of trash cans and his feet grew numb in his boots, the sight of rabbit tracks in fresh snow or raccoons raiding birdfeeders made him feel he had been let in on secrets the sleepers would never know. In summer, when chicken guts and spoiled milk and rotting cabbage stank like the outhouse on his grandparents' farm, the calls of geese and sandhill cranes drifted down from the sky and sunrise filled the streets with gold. In all seasons, Gordon enjoyed breaking the morning silence by banging cans on the edge of the hopper, not because the clanging woke sleepers, but because, in those early hours and empty streets, making so much noise gave him a sense of authority that he felt no other time of day.

If anyone asked Gordon's children what their father did for a living, they would say he was a mechanic at the city garage, that he was a maintenance engineer, that he drove trucks. But they would never admit that, for months at a time when his back was ailing him, their father collected trash. When he trudged home, still wearing his vest with the bright-orange X, none of the kids ran outside to hug him. Mabel insisted that he undress in the garage and put his sour coveralls directly into the wash. The grandparents inspected the junk he had scavenged, on the lookout for antiques, but they avoided talking with him about his smelly work.

As it happened, Gordon's route took him past his own house, and so once a week he got to rouse his family by stopping out front and grinding the hydraulic compactor and banging the trash cans. The only one who ever appeared at a window with an expression other than a frown was Danny, the youngest, who still believed in rising with the sun.

Noticing Danny's grinning face in the kitchen window one morning before sunrise, Zeke remarked to Gordon, "Cute kid."

"He's a keeper, alright. Takes after his mother."

"I never was cute, not even as a little squirt," said Zeke, skidding a can over the pavement. "I know, I've seen the pictures."

In the flashing yellow glow of the truck's hazard lights, Gordon studied his partner, whose thin face looked worn, like the Abe Lincoln on a penny that has tumbled through too many pockets. To see any kid hurting made Gordon wince as he would for his own children. Zeke couldn't be much older than Bruce, maybe a year or two younger than Jeanne.

When the hopper was full, Zeke climbed up front with Gordon, and they drove out to the landfill, passing woods and farms and weedy fields along the way. That was another compensation for the grunt and stink of this job. How many city folks got paid to look at the waking countryside, the circling crows, the grazing cattle? At dawn, even in summer, mist rose from ponds like steam from coffee. Red-tailed hawks hunched on fenceposts, and turkey vultures perched on telephone poles with their wings held out to dry. Deer glanced up from meadows with hanks of grass drooping from their jaws. On those drives to the dump, sometimes Zeke wouldn't say a word, and other times he would talk a blue streak, reciting for Gordon a long history of defeats.

This morning, as they waited their turn to unload at the dump, while bats on their last outings before full daylight crisscrossed in front of the truck hunting for bugs, Gordon asked him why he'd dropped out of school. "Was it too many rules? Empty pockets? Algebra?"

"Naw," said Zeke, "I breezed through algebra. And I could get by without the crummy wages the city pays me. My dad's a deadbeat, but he coughs up enough alimony to keep me and my mom afloat. I didn't hate school or anything; I just felt out of it."

"Out of what?"

"Everything. I never knew which band was hot, never watched the right shows, never wore the trendy clothes, never had the groovy phone. I was too skinny for sports, too ugly for girls."

"Who says you're ugly?"

"The bathroom mirror when I'm brushing my crooked teeth and trying to plaster my fuzzball hair into a shape nobody will laugh at."

Homely since birth, Gordon had never spent much time in front of mirrors. "So that's all?" he said. "You dropped out of school because you didn't make the cool crowd?"

"I didn't make *any* crowd. It's like nobody even saw me. I'd raise my hand in class and teachers never called on me. When I walked down the halls, nobody said, 'Hey, Zeke, what's up?' So I started skipping school, and when I turned eighteen, I quit."

"In your senior year?"

"The summer before."

"You couldn't stick it out one more year to graduate?"

"What the hell for?"

"To get a degree. Maybe go to college. Make something of yourself."

Zeke snorted. "What's there to make, man?"

"Look at me," said Gordon. "I had to take algebra twice, but I didn't quit." Only the first half of this claim was true, since he had quit school at sixteen. But it was okay to stretch the truth now and again, especially with kids, to keep them on the straight and narrow.

"Yeah," said Zeke, "look at you."

Gordon didn't know how to answer that. What had he made of his life? He'd never moved from the town he was born in, had rarely left Indiana except when the navy sent him to the Middle East, where he saw mostly desert and dust, and came back home wondering why people would slaughter one another over such a godforsaken place. He couldn't afford to go away on vacation, not even to the Indiana Dunes, which he'd been wanting to visit since he was a boy. He'd never gone much of anywhere except around in circles, like the wheeling crows, like the garbage truck on its runs between city and dump. He didn't have a dime in savings. The kids would all have to work their way through college, as Jeanne was doing. If anybody got really sick or the grandparents needed surgery, where would he find the money?

"Anyway," said Zeke, "a guy can learn stuff without going to school. I read books and blogs. I watch documentaries on TV. For instance, did you know that scientists figure maybe ninety percent of the mass in the universe is invisible?"

Surveying the mountains of trash, Gordon found this hard to believe. "It is?"

"Nowhere to be seen. Dark matter, they call it."

Gordon let out the clutch, and the truck groaned ahead in line. Away at the edge of the dump, smoke rose from trash fires. "If they can't see it, how do they know it's missing?"

"Because otherwise all the galaxies would fly apart. And the expansion of the universe would be slowing down instead of speeding up."

"So the scientists used to know where all this stuff was, and now they lost track of it?"

"No, see, they only just now figured out it's got to *be* there. They can't detect it, is all. Like, suppose you calculate from the sag on a clothesline that it would take ten pairs of jeans to weight it down like that, but you only see one pair. You know there must be nine more, but they're hidden."

"I'd figure the dog stole them," Gordon said, hoping to cheer up this glum boy.

Instead of chuckling, Zeke groaned. For a while he said nothing, and then he muttered, "Garbage is depressing, you know that?"

"How come?"

"It's all that guys like you and me leave behind, right? I mean, we're never going to write songs that people hum when they do the dishes, are we? Never going to star in a movie. Never going to start a business that keeps making useful stuff after we're gone. Nobody's going to name a scientific discovery after us, or a crater on the moon, or a city street. So all we leave behind is the stuff we break and use up and throw out. Trash, right?"

Gordon looked at the boy's drawn face. "You're way too young to think like that."

Again Zeke let out a breath, and this time he switched off, closing his eyes and tilting his head against the wall of the cab.

They lurched ahead in line. One more truck, and then it would be Gordon's turn to add his load to the trash mountain. He remembered how, back when he was fresh out of the navy and just starting work for the city, from up here he'd glimpsed curtains of light waving on the northern horizon. One morning they'd be blue, another morning yellow or green. He hadn't found anybody else who could see them until he brought Jeanne to have a look. She'd been a toddler back then, and now she was halfway through college, nearly a grown woman, long past thinking that a ride to the dump with Dad was a treat. Over the years, he had brought each of the children in turn, and all of them had opened their eyes wide at the sight, but eventually the novelty wore off, and nowadays only Danny was still eager to come see the lights when they were dancing.

Gordon sensed they might be dancing now, although with his clouded vision he couldn't tell for sure. "Zeke," he said, pointing through the windshield, "look there to the north. Do you see anything shining?"

Grudgingly, the boy opened his eyes. "Headlights on bulldozers shoving garbage back and forth."

"Look higher. Up in the sky."

Zeke lifted his gaze, let out a huff of surprise, and a smile broke over his face. "Oh my God! It's the aurora borealis!"

"The what?"

"Aurora borealis. The northern lights. All those shimmering green curtains. Can't you see them?"

"Not real clear, because of my cataracts."

"Man oh man oh man," Zeke murmured, staring. "The northern lights, blazing down on Indiana. Who would have thought?"

"I was hoping you could see them. I brought all my kids up here to show them when they were little."

"You brought your kids to the dump?"

"Sure. Didn't your dad ever take you places to show you stuff?"

"All my old man ever showed me was a balled-up fist and the door he slammed behind him when he walked out on Mom and me."

Gordon's own fists tightened on the steering wheel, as he imagined what he'd like to say to that father. "How old were you when he left?"

"Eight," Zeke said. "That was ten years ago, and I can still hear the door slam and the tires squealing as he drove away."

"That's a real shame."

"That's history," Zeke said, his gaze still fixed on the horizon. After a spell of silence, he asked, "Why don't you get your eyes fixed? They've got this laser surgery that can clear up your vision like magic."

"Maybe after my kids get through college." To avoid having to admit he didn't have a dime in savings, he said, "With all the reading you do, I bet you could tell me what makes that shimmery glow."

"I could, sure. Photons and molten iron and Earth's magnetic field and all the rest. It's neat stuff. But right now I want to keep quiet and look."

"You do that." Gordon slapped Zeke on the knee. "The world's full of things worth seeing. It's not all garbage."

For the crows, picking over the spoils in search of tidbits to eat, even garbage wasn't garbage, and off in the distance the waking city glowed like a swarm of fireflies. Humming one of his little tunes, Gordon maneuvered the truck into position at the edge of the bulldozed area, lifted the hopper, engaged the hydraulic cylinder to shove the trash out the back, and then eased forward until the box was empty. Turning to Zeke, he said, "Ready for another run, partner?"

"I guess. The lights will be gone before we come back."

"They'll be there other mornings. Just keep your eyes peeled."

"I will."

Gordon kept his own eyes peeled as he drove back into town. Maybe an eagle would fly over from Lake Debs to check out roadkill. Maybe a coyote would lope across a pasture with a rabbit in his jaws. Maybe a black bear would rear up from a ditch to sniff the sweet garbage smell as the truck rolled by. Even if no critters appeared, the woods glowed with early light, and that was reward enough for looking. He thought about how forests grow back on any ground left fallow in these Indiana hills, how each tree puts down roots in one spot and finds everything it needs right there, without budging, and how it grows up and grows old and dies and rots back into the soil, leaving behind maybe a few saplings of its own kind to take their turn in the sun. So what if I haven't traveled much? he thought. So what if I dropped out of school? So what if I haven't saved a dime? I've got four fine children, don't I? They'll get the schooling, they'll do the traveling, maybe they'll have kids of their own and look after Mabel and me in our old age, the way we're looking after our old folks. And there's Mabel, too, a woman I've loved every minute of every day for a quarter century, and, wonder of wonders, she loves me back. She rubs my body where it aches, and I rub hers. She's good at her work, and I'm good at mine, and between us we've kept our family going. That all adds up to something, doesn't it?

Alligators

*V*isitors from the metropolis are often surprised to learn that indoor toilets have been adopted throughout the Midwest, even in the hills of southern Indiana. Septic systems are the rule in the countryside, and sewers in the cities. Old-timers don't miss having to visit the privy in the dark of night, especially in the dead of winter through a foot of snow when icicles hang from the outhouse roof, but they do miss seeing the stars while trudging there and back, miss hearing owls while going about their business, and miss having occasion to read the Sears & Roebuck catalog, a privy amenity that also provided a handy source of toilet paper. Nowadays, sitting on the pot indoors, folks have nothing to hear but the body's own ruckus or the house's wooden groans, and nothing to see but wallpaper or cracked plaster, and no catalogs to read since all the merchants moved their wares online. On balance, though, even the old-timers admit that indoor plumbing marks an improvement over outhouses, but it does have one major drawback, which is that subterranean pipes and sewage lagoons offer ideal habitat for alligators.

How the first alligators reached Limestone, Indiana, was a matter of debate in the household of Gordon and Mabel Mills. The grandparents believed the beasts must have stowed away in Hoosier automobiles returning from Florida vacations. The two Mills boys, who loved to swim, imagined the alligators might have paddled upstream from the Gulf of Mexico, curious to see more of the country. Veronica suggested that baby gators might have been sold in pet stores mislabeled as lizards. Jeanne, drawing on what she had learned in college about climate chaos, argued that tropical species were ranging into higher latitudes as northern waters warmed. Gordon was partial to a theory he'd heard on the radio, which claimed that sandhill cranes had carried alligator eggs for snacks on their northward migration and accidentally dropped a few in the wastewater treatment tanks. Mabel declared herself agnostic on the subject. She didn't care how these monsters had begun breeding in the sewers; she wanted them cleared out, so a person could sit on a toilet without fearing that a toothy green snout might take a bite out of her posterior.

Workers at the treatment plant offered eyewitness accounts of the alligators as well as photos, which appeared on the front page of the *Limestone Tribune*, accompanied by grim headlines: FANGED MONSTERS UNDER OUR FEET, for instance, or CRUEL KILLERS PROWL PIPES. A local preacher identified the beasts as a cross between Leviathan and Behemoth, sure signs of the apocalypse as foretold in the Book of Revelations and a warning to his congregation that they should pray fervently and double their tithing if they wanted to assure themselves a place in the Rapture. The Tourist Bureau debated whether to bill the alligators as a wildlife attraction but decided that the sewage lagoon, the prime viewing area, would not be the most salubrious destination for visitors. The Chamber of Commerce offered a bounty for alligator hides, which would be turned into purses by children in Bangladesh and then sold to raise money for the Limestone Boys & Girls Club. But no one dared to hunt the gators, not even the police, who cited union rules prohibiting the shooting of animals within city limits. This left the citizens to fend for themselves. The big box stores advertised cans of pepper spray for self-defense, to be kept handy in the bathroom. The Rotary Club donated slingshots to schoolchildren. Folks old enough to remember midnight trips to the outhouse and other country ways recommended wearing necklaces of garlic to ward off attacks.

None of these developments reassured Mabel. No matter how many times Gordon explained that an alligator larger than a salamander couldn't slither through the maze of plumbing into a toilet bowl, she was not appeased. Never shy about expressing her views, she confronted the mayor one Saturday morning at the farmers' market, demanding that he do something about the plague of reptiles. The mayor didn't want to lose his place in line at the booth with the premier sweet corn, so he had to stand there while Mabel Mills—a woman whom he knew only too well from previous kerfuffles—gave him an earful about rabies, tetanus, sleeping sickness, nervous bowels, lost limbs, and other dangers posed by alligators. As a crowd gathered, echoing her complaints, the mayor vowed to address the problem Monday morning.

True to his word, first thing on Monday he called the public works director, who called the maintenance supervisor, who called Gordon, who was scheduled to drive a street sweeper on the graveyard shift.

"Change of plan, Mills," the supervisor told him over the phone. "Instead of cleaning the streets, you're going to get rid of the alligators."

"How am I supposed to do that?" Gordon asked.

"However you want. Just so they're gone by next weekend."

"Why next weekend?"

"Because the mayor wants to shop at the farmers' market without getting hassled by your wife."

As Gordon left for work that evening, he didn't mention his new assignment to Mabel, who tended to imagine the worst outcome from any situation, which in this case would be for an alligator to eat her husband. Not a worrier himself, Gordon drove slowly to the maintenance garage, mulling over plans. Everyone else on the graveyard shift was told to give him whatever help he needed and otherwise to leave him alone, an order that prompted the crew to razz Gordon when he arrived. Without responding to their malarkey, he walked straight into the machine shop and closed the door. Every now and again, he came back out to fetch a tool or rummage through the supply shelves for parts. Otherwise, all that emerged from the shop were sounds—the whir of a saw, the pop of a riveting gun, the sizzle of a welding torch. At the end of the shift, out he came, posted a DO NOT DISTURB sign on the door, and marched away lugging his lunch box, not saying a word about what he was up to.

Tuesday night was the same, and Wednesday night as well. At the start of graveyard shift on Thursday, the supervisor intercepted Gordon and demanded to know why he hadn't so much as opened a manhole cover or poked around in the sewers. "While you're tinkering in the shop, Mills, alligators are terrorizing the city."

Gordon merely waved him aside and asked for a case of green spray paint. The paint was delivered, along with a stern reminder from the supervisor about the mayor's weekend deadline.

As the sun rose on Friday, the shop door sprang open and out rolled a machine shaped like a sea monster on wheels, with headlights for eyes, tailpipes for nostrils, hubcaps for scales, and a propeller at the tip of its tail. It was heavily armored and painted end to end a glossy green. Through a window in the forehead of the beast peered Gordon's grinning face.

"Mills, you've got to be kidding," the supervisor shouted. "How's that going to clean out the sewers?"

The jaws opened, revealing teeth made of knife blades and a tongue bristling with spikes, and from a loudspeaker in the throat came Gordon's growl: "Haul me to the sewage lagoon and you'll see."

The supervisor himself hauled Gordon and his sea monster to the treatment plant on a flatbed truck and lowered the contraption with a crane into the murky water. Soon a small alligator swam up, took one look at the green monster, and fled with a thrashing of its tail. A second alligator did the same, then a third and a fourth, each one larger than the one before, but none daring to challenge this intruder. The parade continued until the lagoon was filled with a raft of reptiles, all milling about at a wary distance.

Finally the biggest and fiercest of the whole tribe showed up, loosed a defiant roar, and charged at Gordon's machine with jaws agape. Suddenly the headlights flashed, the loudspeaker boomed, and out of the nostrils poured a cloud of steam, which blinded the alligator king just long enough for the sea monster to ram him in the ribs, bite him on the snout, and flip him into the air. As soon as the great beast hit the water, he struck out for shore, scrambled onto the bank, and hightailed it for the nearest creek.

Every last alligator in the city hurried after him, and off they fled downstream, from Geode Creek into the White River, then along the Wabash, the Ohio, and the Mississippi, slowing down only when they reached the bayous of Louisiana. Rumors of their narrow escape spread along the Gulf Coast, from one reptilian clan to the next, and with each retelling the green monster grew more terrible. Since that time, no alligator has troubled Gordon's hometown—or any other place in Indiana, so far as we've heard.

At the farmers' market on the day after the last alligator fled south, the mayor waited in the sweet corn line hoping that Mabel Mills would not show up to complain about some other matter and embarrass him in front of potential voters. When Mabel did show up, instead of complaining, she greeted the mayor cheerily and thanked him for planning to offer city employees a 5 percent raise, increase the library budget, offer curbside recycling pickup, install solar panels on all public buildings, and restore art classes in the schools. The mayor had no such plans, but he could not say so outright, since other marketgoers, overhearing Mabel's words, began clustering around her and adding their own support to these initiatives. "A living wage!" somebody said.

And others cried, "Renewable energy!" "Extend library hours!" "Ban plastic bags!" "We need art!"

Then a child's voice piped up: "Put the Great Gator Gizmo on the courthouse square!"

Nodding thoughtfully, the mayor took a notepad out of his pocket and wrote down these suggestions, reserving judgment on all of them except the last, the only one that would not cost taxpayer dollars. Yes, indeed, he promised, the ingenious device that banished the alligators shall be exhibited for a full month on the courthouse square.

This announcement drew cheers from the crowd, much to the mayor's relief and Danny's delight. For the child's voice belonged to Danny, who had nicknamed his dad's invention the Great Gator Gizmo—or G cubed, for short. He had also prompted his mom to call for an increase in the library budget, just as Jeanne had called for curbside recycling pickup, Bruce had come up with the solar panel suggestion, and Veronica had championed art in the schools. Mabel's wily appeal to the mayor was a family affair.

And so it came to pass that Gordon's cobbled-together machine took its place on the courthouse lawn, between the war memorial and the peace monument. Except for the jaws, which he had bolted shut to keep the sharp teeth out of reach, every part of the Great Gator Gizmo was open to inspection by the curious, from the propeller at the tip of the tail to the grass-green snout. Children were fond of climbing inside, closing the hatch, and making goofy faces at their friends who stared in through the windshield. Of course parents and grandparents couldn't resist taking snapshots of all those playful kids, nor could they resist posting these photos on social media, including images taken at angles that emphasized the machine's resemblance to a sea monster. Within hours, the Indiana Visitors Bureau began circulating news and images of the Great Gator Gizmo as yet another reason to come spend time and money in the Hoosier State.

The mayor often stopped by the display during his lunch hour to accept congratulations for having commissioned such a clever solution to the plague of alligators. The director of public works occasionally showed up, as well, along with the maintenance supervisor, both of whom accepted thanks while pointing out that the real credit should go to the loyal city employee, Gordon Mills. Needless to say, Gordon avoided the spotlight. When reporters for the *Limestone Tribune* and *Indianapolis Star* called the Mills house, asking to speak with him, the family made up excuses for why he couldn't come to the phone. When TV crews showed up at the front door, he fled out the back.

The reporters redoubled their efforts to interview the elusive Gordon Mills after the governor announced that the Great Gator Gizmo would be shipped to Indianapolis following its month on the courthouse square and would be put on permanent display at the State Museum, as another demonstration of Hoosier ingenuity exemplified by the biplanes of the Wright brothers, the classy cars of the Studebaker brothers, the mechanical corn picker, gas pump, canning jars, transistor radio, rubber-soled sneakers, and other examples too numerous to mention. It was even rumored that the governor might name Gordon Mills a Sagamore of the Wabash, the state's highest honor for service to the public.

Unable to reach this potential Sagamore by phone or at his home, newspaper sleuths and TV crews finally tracked him down at the city maintenance garage. Once Gordon realized they would not quit pestering him until he gave them a few words for their cameras and notepads, he gathered his thoughts, scratched his beard, and said, "I've got nothing against alligators, which are amazing creatures, and I hope there's always swampy places where they can live out their lives in peace and raise up their young, just so long as it's not in the sewers of my hometown." As he finished his little speech, and before the reporters could ask him any more questions, he said politely, "Now if you folks will excuse me, I've got to get back to work." And back to work he went.

Worry

No matter how tired he was from his daylong tussle with the city's broken machines, Gordon could never go to bed until all of his children had come safely home from their evening prowls. The youngest of the four kids, golden-haired Danny, not yet allowed to roam at night, was no cause for worry. But who knew what might happen to the other three, out there in the darkness? His older son might fall prey to other men's daughters, his daughters to other men's sons. A gang might jump them. A druggie might slip them a pill or jab them with a needle. They might get hit by lightning or falling trees. Rats with rabies could rush from sewers and bite them. On the highway, a drunk in a hot rod or a dozing trucker might swerve across the center line and clobber them. They might be scorched in a fire, swept up in a mob of protesters, or snatched away by a tornado.

"Fat lot of good your worrying will do," Mabel often reminded him, with an exasperation only slightly dulled by twenty-five years of marriage.

"You get your beauty sleep, pigeon," Gordon would reply. "I'll be along in a bit."

Then he would stay up imagining calamities long after Mabel had gone down grumbling to their musty bedroom in the basement. He puttered in the garage, sorting nuts and bolts into jars, or he pored over seed catalogues at the kitchen table, or he stretched out on the living room couch and skimmed the newspaper, glancing every now and again at the muted TV, where painted faces opened and closed their mouths like tropical fish. All the while he kept an ear cocked for the rattle of the front door.

Ordinarily, he wasn't a worrying sort of man. His buddies at the city garage liked to pull jobs with him because no matter how fast things were falling apart, Gordon's hands never shook and his head never came unscrewed. His command of tools and the calm in his broad homely face took the urgency out of burst water mains and fried circuits and stalled trucks. "No sweat," he would say, rolling up his sleeves. By day's end those sleeves and the rest of his shirt and every stitch of clothing he had on would be soggy with sweat, but it was the sweat of overheated muscles, not of nerves.

Little in this chancy world had caused Gordon to fret until the night when Mabel delivered their first baby, a mewling girl with curly hair the color of a fox's pelt. Gordon bent down until his ear nearly brushed the baby's lips, listening for breath, and what he heard was a tiny voice whispering, "Don't ever let anything hurt me." That daughter, Jeanne, was now a sophomore in college, her red hair cut short and her face bare of makeup so as to discourage romance, and still the boys trailed after her with hungry eyes.

During the nineteen years since Jeanne's birth, Gordon had winced every time he imagined any of his children suffering harm.

All one summer, the child who made him lose the most sleep was Bruce, their aspiring astrophysicist and tech wizard, who was saving up for college by working the evening shift at a pizza joint. "Making dough to make dough," Bruce liked to say. Finished at eleven, he usually came home before twelve, which was bad enough, since Gordon's alarm would go off at five. Then the boy started coming in later and later, well past midnight, past one, past two. Waiting up for him, Gordon imagined enough disasters to fill the evening news for a month.

"Overtime," was all Bruce would say when he finally arrived.

Gordon was so relieved to see the big galoot come home in one piece that he didn't push him for an explanation. Might as well try to squeeze a song out of a pillow as try to squeeze words out of a teenager. Besides, noticing the chapped lips and bloodshot eyes, Gordon could guess what had been keeping the boy out so late. Necking was fine, necking was natural. No doubt Adam and Eve smooched in the garden, even before they realized they were naked. Kissing was risky, of course, but it wouldn't hurt you so long as you kept your zipper zipped. The question was, did Bruce and the girl, whoever she might be, know when to stop?

Then one morning when Bruce wandered in at three, Gordon woke from a snooze on the couch, beat away the newspaper that had collapsed over his face, and before he could stop himself, he muttered, "If you get her in trouble, I'll break your skull."

"Her who?" said Bruce. "What trouble?"

Coming fully awake, Gordon felt he should soften his words. "I'm not saying you can't enjoy yourself. But just remember where kissing leads to."

Tall, pale-skinned, too handsome ever to be taken for a son of the dark and dumpy Gordon Mills, Bruce was also shy. For years he had built up a science of girls in his head, studying their moods and moves, but his knowledge of how to actually behave with them, especially in those scary stages beyond kissing, was sketchier than his knowledge of differential calculus.

"I haven't been hanging around with a girl, Dad."

"Then how'd your lips get so raw?"

Bruce raked the back of a wrist across his mouth. "Not from nibbling females."

"So what *have* you been doing after work?"

"Nothing."

"Nothing? You stay out half the night doing nothing?"

"You wouldn't understand," said Bruce. For about three years now, this had been the boy's guiding conviction—that Gordon, immune to poetry and passion, a battered old workhorse with a tenth-grade education, a relic from some earlier stage in evolution, couldn't fathom anything of interest to a modern teenager. "Believe me, Pops, it wouldn't make any sense to you."

"Try me," Gordon said.

Bruce released a hissing breath, which was his way of saying, "Here goes nothing." "Okay. I was hacking."

The word made Gordon think of butchers, muggers, clumsy carpenters. "Hacking what?"

"You know, working on a computer. The manager lets me use his laptop after Mama Panda's Pizza closes."

Gordon could decipher the workings of any machine that possessed a motor and gears, but the few times he'd looked inside a computer, nothing made sense to him except the fan. "You're keeping the books?" he asked. "Doing one of those spreadsheet things?"

"No, I'm just coding," Bruce said, running his tongue over his lips. "Making up worlds, creating avatars, that sort of thing."

"Messing around?"

"If you want to call it that." Bruce turned away, sulking, then spun around to add: "I *said* you wouldn't understand."

But to Gordon, the pleasure of messing around with machines—souping up cars, tuning motorcycles, restoring player pianos—made perfect sense, even if he didn't know beans about computers. Remembering how the passion for tinkering had first gripped him as a boy, when he built a shortwave radio out of parts he'd scavenged from junked appliances at the dump, Gordon found it hard to say no a few days later when Bruce proposed tapping into his savings to buy the components for a computer.

"If I put it together myself, it's cheaper than getting a prebuilt," Bruce pointed out. "And I can customize it to suit my interests."

Gordon scratched his beard, thinking of how much he had learned from building machines, studying how they worked, taking them apart, and rebuilding them. "Like what interests?"

"Simulations, animations, gaming, art. Lots of things. Besides," Bruce added, "everybody I know already has a computer."

"Everybody you know comes from a family with more money than we've got and fewer mouths to feed."

"I'll need one anyhow when I start college."

"That's two years away."

"But if I get my own system now, I won't have to stay out late using the laptop at the store. And you won't have to fall asleep on the couch worrying about me."

That clinched the deal.

When the parts arrived, Gordon offered to help put them together, figuring he could learn right along with Bruce while they assembled the mother board, processor, power supply, and other pieces of the puzzle. Bruce said thanks but no thanks. Lugging the boxes, he disappeared into the attic bedroom he shared with Danny.

Soon Danny came jouncing down the stairs carrying an armful of plastic dinosaurs. Finding Gordon writing checks at the kitchen table, he announced, "Big Bro kicked me out. He's got a bug up his wazoo."

"Watch your mouth," Gordon said, trying to sound gruff. "Ladies might be listening."

"Ladies never heard of wazoos? How about if I say Brucie's got a bug up his bum?"

"Scram," Gordon said, peeling another bill from the stack.

For the next three days, while the sounds of whistling filled the attic, Danny was exiled to the screened porch, and Bruce only emerged from the room every few hours or so to raid the kitchen, his bleary eyes fixed on some inner diagram, his lips cracked from nervous licking. He forgot his job at the pizza joint. When the manager called, Mabel told him the boy had come down with a fever, which was true after a fashion. Talking with Bruce during his food excursions was pointless, a fact that did not keep Gordon from asking how the computer was coming along nor keep Mabel from urging him to get more rest. Bruce mumbled unintelligible answers, his mouth stuffed with bagels or bananas or salami sandwiches.

On the fourth day, the manager of Mama Panda's Pizza called to say that Bruce was fired.

"You didn't pay him enough anyway, you skinflint," Mabel told him over the phone.

Early on the fifth day, Bruce let out a triumphant yell that woke the girls on the second floor, the grandparents on the ground floor, Danny on the foldout bed on the porch, and Mabel and Gordon in the basement. In pajamas and robes and fuzzy slippers, the family rushed to see what was up, and they found Bruce tapping the keys of the finished computer, his eyes fixed on the screen where pictures and words flickered in eerie green light.

"Come on, baby," he murmured, "come on, you darling."

Those were among the few words anyone heard him speak until a week later, when the hum of not one but two voices filtered through his perpetually closed door. To the astonishment of Gordon and Mabel, who had crept up the attic stairway to listen, the second of those voices sounded like a girl.

"Can you believe it," Mabel whispered, "our shy Brucie?"

"How did he sneak her in?" said Gordon.

"She must be a brazen hussy to force herself on our innocent boy!"

"Might do him some good. Draw him out of his shell."

Mabel pressed her ear to the door. "I just hope and pray he remembers where kissing leads to."

"It's only natural," Gordon said.

"So are babies and heartache and disease," Mabel said, growing more agitated by the second. "We've got to break this up before it gets serious."

Gordon rapped on the door, then paused, wanting to give the couple time to adjust their clothing, if need be. The two voices chatted on, one of them Bruce's familiar baritone and the other a sultry soprano. Cautiously, Gordon opened the door a crack and peeked inside, uneasy about what he might see. There sat Bruce staring at the computer screen, where a girl's face glimmered, her skin the color of butterscotch, her raven black hair a tumble of curls that threw off sparks as she moved, her lips a glossy pink. The motion of those lips and the voice purring from the speakers were not quite synchronized, as in a foreign movie with English poorly dubbed.

As Gordon and Mabel crept into the room, the girl was saying, " . . . ruffled parasols, although sunbonnets or palm branches will also do."

"And if it rains?" said Bruce.

"Umbrellas," said the girl on the screen. "Slickers and galoshes, depending on the force and duration, and then rowboats, submarines, arks."

"And for snow?"

"Long underwear, wool socks, boots, down-filled coats. Hot chocolate. All manner of fires."

"For boredom?"

"Books and flowers and the night sky."

"For the blues?"

"Banjos and yo-yos."

"For loneliness?"

"Love."

Mabel didn't like the drift of this, nor did she like the looks of the flirt on the screen or the hollows in her son's cheeks. "Brucie? Sweetie?"

"Hey, buddy," Gordon said. "Hey, big guy." It required the firm squeeze of his hand on the boy's shoulder to break into this entranced dialogue.

Bruce looked up with bloodshot eyes. "Huh?"

"Aren't you going to introduce us to your friend?"

Since the boy just sat there, mum, Mabel addressed the screen. "Hello, there. We're Bruce's parents. Would you mind telling us who you are?" The girl did not reply, and her face seemed to freeze.

"You're wasting your breath, Mom," said Bruce, explaining that the image on the screen was an avatar, the product of an animation generator and a voice synthesizer and thousands of lines of code. He threw out a good many other terms that whizzed right by Gordon and Mabel—CPUs, frame rate, jump cuts, terminal errors, incremental loops, terabytes—all the while licking his lips from excitement. They understood for sure only that the girl's name was Miranda.

"She's like a ventriloquist's dummy?" Gordon suggested. "You're just feeding her words?"

"Nope," said Bruce. "The program is self-revising, changing parameters, searching memory banks, growing up. It's so complicated, I never know what Miranda's going to say."

"You quit a good job to sit up all night yakking with a machine?" said Mabel.

"She understands me."

Mabel rolled her eyes. "She understands you, but you don't understand her?"

This contradiction did not puzzle Gordon, for whom girls and women had always seemed opaque, while he felt himself to be transparent before their x-ray eyes. He checked out the image on the screen, the hair like a storm cloud, the eyes the color of grass, the butterscotch skin. She

126

wasn't the type he would fall for, nothing at all like Mabel, but he could see that for Bruce she might be Miss Universe.

"You'll ruin your health," said Mabel. "You'll strain your eyes."

Instead of answering, Bruce dove back into his dialogue with the phantom girl.

Miranda's voice became as familiar in the house as the gurgle of the plumbing and the wheeze of the window fans. She laughed, she sighed, she lectured, she moaned. For long stretches she never spoke louder than a whisper, and then suddenly she would shout, sob, or break into song. Bruce, meanwhile, coaxed and cooed. The two sisters were embarrassed by this schmaltzy drama, Danny thought it was just plain dumb, and the grandparents considered it one more sign that the younger generation had gone completely haywire. In their basement bedroom, Gordon and Mabel could hear the sugary tones seeping down through the heating ducts.

This continued for several weeks—night after night of sandbag sleep for Gordon, who didn't have to wonder what Bruce might be doing outside in the treacherous dark, and night after night of fretful tossing for Mabel.

"This is getting scary," she said one evening at bedtime.

"It's only make-believe," said Gordon.

"It's unnatural."

"He'll grow out of it."

"Why doesn't he find a real girl?"

The answer came to Gordon swiftly: "Because the real ones spook him."

The family woke up early the next Saturday to the noise of a quarrel rattling the attic. For an hour or so, the house throbbed with shouts.

Bruce would holler, then Miranda, then both at once. Gordon wanted to go referee, but Mabel said, "No, let them fight it out."

By midmorning, the attic was silent, and then at noon to everyone's amazement Bruce came downstairs for lunch, fresh from the shower, wearing a clean T-shirt and jeans, shaved for the first time in days, his hair combed into neat rows. His sleepless eyes were glazed with bewilderment. In a trembling voice, he announced that he had broken up with Miranda.

From their seats around the table, the other members of the family stared at him with a mixture of sympathy and relief.

"It's probably for the best," said Mabel, who knew it was absolutely for the best.

"Now maybe I can move back into my room," Danny said.

"Love is a trap anyhow," said Jeanne, who had shorn her foxy curls in an effort to fend off male pursuers.

"She kept talking about other guys, movie stars and rappers," Bruce explained. "So I called it quits."

"You erased her?" Gordon asked.

"I couldn't go that far," Bruce replied, frowning at his split pea soup. "So I saved her to the cloud."

During the afternoon, while everyone else was away from the house, Gordon and Bruce tuned up the lawnmower, the first time they had worked together in ages. Bucked up by this, Gordon suggested that when the mower was finished, they should play a game of catch. Neither one could remember where the baseball gloves were, so Bruce went inside to look.

"Try my dad's sea trunk, up under the eaves," Gordon called after him.

Half an hour passed, and Bruce didn't return. Gordon stuck his head in the kitchen, but before he could yell, "Hey, buddy!" he was silenced by the sound of sobs leaking down from the attic. He kicked off his boots and crept upstairs as quietly as his clunky feet would allow. The weeping voice was so broken, he couldn't decide whether it belonged to Miranda or to Bruce.

The door to the attic bedroom stood open. Gordon, his oily hands curled into fists, gazed in helplessly at his son, who sat before the blank computer screen, head thrown back, wailing. The baseball gloves lay forgotten in his lap. Such pain under my own roof, thought Gordon. Why doesn't it come for me instead of my boy?

Wolf

For Veronica, age twelve, it was a season of tears, most of them set flowing by her father. Could any other dad be so hairy or clumsy or loud? His beard was a wiry thicket, which he scratched like a dog scratching fleas. Even when he shaved, his jowls were stained with shadow, and by suppertime the black whiskers made him look like something escaped from the zoo. Hair spread down his neck, over his shoulders, across his back and chest, curly black fur streaked with gray. His legs were unspeakable, thick and fuzzy and knotted with muscle. Yet in summer he would mow the front lawn wearing only plaid Bermuda shorts, where anybody who passed by the house could see, and even in winter, home from his job at the city garage, he would strip off his filthy coveralls at the door and parade to the bathroom in his long johns.

As her father tramped through the house, he was sure to jostle a table or thump against a chair. True, his big hands were surprisingly deft, and Veronica would go to him rather than her mother to have the clasp on a necklace replaced or a splinter removed. But those hands seemed to have drained all the grace from the rest of his body. Built like a muskox, broad and heavy, he made the floorboards groan, and the breeze stirred up by his passing would tumble vases and slam doors.

From her bedroom upstairs, Veronica could follow his lumbering movements by the racket he made.

Little of the racket came from talking, because he rarely had much to say, and for that Veronica was grateful. But when he did speak, his voice erupted like the backfire of a truck. Even with his mouth shut he still made noises, grunting as he read the paper, snorting as he lowered himself into a chair, or humming for no reason at all.

The humming was especially irksome to Veronica in that spring of her thirteenth year. After much begging, she had finally persuaded her folks to pay for ballet lessons. How could she fill her soul with real music when her father hummed snatches of folk songs and jukebox tunes and country ballads, a few notes over and over again, never finishing the melody, his voice as rumbly as old plumbing? Most of the time he didn't even realize he was humming, for when she pleaded with him, tears running down her cheeks, "Stop it, Daddy, you're driving me nuts!" he would gape at her, startled, then clench his jaw.

Studying ballet was crucial to Veronica's master plan, which aimed at making her poised and powerful, the kind of woman who inspires comparisons with goddesses. She knew from novels and films that such magnificent women existed; she had seen photographs of them in magazines and interviews with them on television, although she had never actually met one in her Indiana hometown. Her mom was a wonder, of course, but not what you'd call glamorous. And her older sister, Jeanne, took pains to hide her beauty, most recently by chopping her hair short and dying it green.

For the near term, Veronica hoped the dance lessons would help her land a part in her middle school's production of *Peter and the Wolf.* When she did land a part, she received the news with mixed emotions. Hoping that people would think of swans when they saw her move, she was let down at first to learn that she had been cast in the role of the duck. Still, at least she had a part, and not a male part, either. Other girls were forced to play the hunters, the grandfather, and even Peter, since only one boy auditioned, Turk Richards, and he was chosen to play the wolf.

The April afternoon when he first laid eyes on Turk Richards, Gordon had come home late again from the city garage, where he was working all the overtime he could get in order to pay for those dance lessons. Gordon sat on the back steps in his boxer shorts, trying to cool off before his shower, the sodden coveralls in a heap at his feet. A screen door separated him from the kitchen, where Mabel—who always worked overtime, as she pointed out—was listening to a radio program about earthquakes while skinning chickens for supper. Every now and again she would call out something to him, but the radio muffled her words, so Gordon would humph in reply, which was usually all the encouragement she needed to continue whatever she was saying.

After putting the chickens in the oven, Mabel came to the door, handed him a carrot, and said, "Did you know we're living right on top of a fault?"

Since coming to consciousness along about age twelve or thirteen, Gordon had been aware of living atop a whole mess of faults—hungers and fears that split him into aching chunks. Mabel was thinking about earthquakes, he realized, so he took a chomp of carrot and said, "Is that a fact?"

"There was a geologist from the college on here saying Indiana only seems to be stable," Mabel reported, "when really we're sitting on a continental plate that's cracked all the way through. Last time it shifted, two centuries ago, the ground rippled for five hundred miles and the Mississippi River ran upstream."

"I suppose we're about due for another one," Gordon said, not knowing why else they would be bringing all this up on the radio.

"That's what this geologist figures."

"Something new to keep you awake at night."

"I'm only telling you what this guy said."

The carrot was bitter, but Gordon kept on gnawing because Mabel wanted him to increase his fiber intake and decrease his bulk. "Is it you that smells so good," he asked her, "or is it your cooking?"

"And if the big one comes," said Mabel, ignoring the detour, "he says our kind of house is about the most dangerous." She tapped a finger against the doorjamb. "It's bad to have two stories, since the top floor can crush you, and brittle old wood is likely to collapse, and a limestone foundation can shiver apart, letting the whole place tumble, plus we've got these huge old shade trees to fall on us and power lines hanging everywhere."

"Good thing you're not the worrying type," Gordon said, a joke that went back to their first meeting, when he saw her car pulled off the highway with a flat tire and he stopped to see if he could lend a hand, and he found her sitting in the driver's seat, gripping the lug wrench, ready to brain him if he made a false move.

"I was just being cautious, in case you turned out to be a creep," she replied with a laugh. "Forewarned is forearmed."

Gordon leaned back from his seat on the steps and growled up at her: "Come on out here, girl, and I'll put a forearm around you."

"Not until you scrub off that grease."

Just then there was a grinding sound along the sidewalk that led to the back door, and from around the corner of the house rolled a boy on a skateboard. He swerved to a halt near the steps, flipped the skateboard into the air with the toe of his black high-top shoe, caught the board neatly, and balanced it on his shoulder, the prow jutting up like the fin of a shark.

"You must be the parentals," he said to Mabel and Gordon.

"How's that?" Gordon said.

"You're Ronnie's folks, hey?" The boy grinned, showing a set of teeth bright and straight enough, Gordon reckoned, to have put an orthodontist's kid through college. "You have that protective look," the boy said. "She here?"

"She's doing homework," Gordon said.

"I'll go see if she's finished," Mabel said. Turning away, she told Gordon, "Better shake a leg. Those chickens have got a head start on you."

"Be right in," he said, but did not budge. He sat there blocking the door, staring at this intruder. There were more troubling things about the boy than Gordon could take in all at once, from the black jeans studded with rivets, to the purple shirt with a white skull on the front, the snake tattoo on one cheek, the silver rings in both ears, on up to the greasy brown hair that stood straight up as if the kid had his finger stuck in a power outlet.

"I hear you're an engineer," the skateboarder said.

"Her name's Veronica," Gordon said.

"That so? Everybody at school calls her Ronnie."

"Her name's Veronica, and I'm no engineer. I'm a mechanic." Gordon balled his hands into fists, the knuckles raw from another day of scraping against the innards of broken machines. "And who're you?"

"He's Turk, Daddy," Veronica said, as she opened the screen door and eased past Gordon down the stairs. "We're in the ballet together."

"Ballet?"

"You know, *Peter and the Wolf.* Didn't I tell you about it? Turk's the wolf, and I'm the duck."

"And I get to eat her up," the boy said. Again he showed those expensive teeth.

Gordon rose heavily to his feet. "You what?"

"Daddy," Veronica broke in, "Mom says you're going to ruin supper if you don't get cleaned up right away."

Gordon's hands felt hot and heavy and useless. He wanted to tell the kid to climb back on the skateboard and beat it. But from the way Veronica glared at him, he knew that if he said one more word or stood there one second longer, she would cry, and if she cried he'd feel rotten for a week. So he clamped his mouth shut, opened the door, and headed for the shower. From behind he could hear the two of them laughing, and the boy saying, "I see what you mean about the paterfamilias."

Give him time, and Gordon could solve almost any problem he could touch. Show him a furniture ad, and he could build a chair or a chest of drawers to match the picture. Bring him a gadget, and if it had moving parts, he would explain how it worked. He could dismantle a wheezing engine, piece by slippery piece, and then fit everything back together again so that it ran like a creek. He could stitch up a dog's torn skin, stop a leak in the toilet, undo the tightest knot, or knead giggles from a baby. One of his reasons for loving babies and toddlers, in fact, was that most of their miseries could be cured by the laying on of hands.

The miseries of teenagers were beyond his reach, however. His oldest child, Jeanne, now at the tail end of her teen years, had proven that, and so had Bruce, who was in the middle of those bewildering years, and now Veronica was just beginning, and there was little Danny to follow. At seven, Danny was still a pretty straightforward kid. Gordon could joke with him, sing to him, tousle his hair, and tell him when to go to bed, how to behave at the table, what shoes to wear to church, all without provoking a tantrum or a sulk.

But dealing with the older three, especially Veronica, was like driving on ice. Gordon would ask her a question or touch a curl in her lustrous black hair or grumble an opinion about the length of her skirt, and suddenly Veronica's face would twist with pain, tears would come, and he would feel himself skidding, out of control, not daring to hit the gas pedal or brake, merely hanging on and hoping to reach clear pavement before the crash.

Trying to find out from Veronica about this Turk Richards was the slickest patch of road that Gordon had come to yet. He couldn't even say the boy's name without stirring up a mist in Veronica's eyes. Almost every afternoon, through the rest of April and into May, the skateboard would come grating down the street, up the driveway and sidewalk, to the back door. Always the back, as if this were a speakeasy or a cat-house. The grinding of those wheels seemed to roll right up Gordon's spine. Veronica would rush downstairs, slow at the door, then glide outside, where she and Turk Richards would sit on the grass and talk in whispers interrupted by sharp bursts of laughter.

"Worrying is my department," Mabel reminded Gordon one night as they were shedding their clothes for bed.

"And chasing thugs from the door is mine," he answered.

"He's just a seventh-grade boy who's gone daft over a pretty girl. He'll get over it, and so will she."

Gordon stood holding his rumpled shirt. "Why does he have to ride that skateboard?"

"Because it's quicker than walking," Mabel said, "and because he's practicing."

"For what?"

"For becoming a professional skateboarder when he grows up. That's why he's in the ballet, according to Veronica. To improve his balance."

"How come she always tells you things and not me?"

"Because I never ask."

"Great, just great. My girl's taken up with a kid who thinks he's going to earn a living by rolling around on a plank."

"They're only twelve years old, sweetheart. Don't you remember being that age, never knowing what you'll feel next, like a pond full of jumping fish?"

Gordon loosened his belt, stepped out of his jeans, but was too worked up to enjoy the smack of night air on his sagging belly. "Every time I hear that skateboard," he said, "I want to grab him and throw him into the next county."

"If you need to throw something," Mabel said, "throw those socks in the mending."

Gordon looked down at his feet and saw both of his big toes poking from the white socks. He felt a sliver of guilt to be making more work for Mabel, but he couldn't help that his toenails were as hard and sharp as chips of flint. Nor could he help wanting to mangle this boy who kept prowling around his daughter.

After mending the socks, Mabel dyed them orange to serve as feet for the duck outfit. She persuaded Gordon to surrender his long-billed painter's cap, and this she also dyed orange, to suggest the duck's head and beak. From Mamaw Hawkins, she borrowed a pair of church gloves, which would turn Veronica's hands into the snowy tips of wings. Except for the leotard, bought from the store, Mabel sewed the remainder of the costume from old sheets or curtain lining, the fabric bleached white enough, as Veronica specified, to make the audience wonder if this duck might after all be a swan in disguise.

Veronica wept in front of the hallway mirror when she first tried on the outfit. The bill of the cap put her face in shadow. The starched gauze of the tutu flaring out from her waist looked like a ring of fog around the moon. The pale top showed the embarrassing new bumps on her chest, and the tights revealed every knob of her knees. The orange socks, rising halfway up her calves, turned her legs into sweet potatoes, and the church gloves practically shouted of grandmothers.

"No, no," Veronica sobbed. "I'm never going to let people see me like this."

"You're gorgeous," Mabel said.

"I look like a reject from cartoons."

"Go ask Bruce or Jeanne. Ask Danny. They'll say how beautiful you are."

"They'll roll on the floor."

"Go ask Dad."

"What does he know?' Veronica moaned through her tears. "He's got about as much sense of style as those manikins in the Salvation Army windows."

"Well," said Mabel, "you can always dance naked. That would cause a stir."

"Mom, that's disgusting!" Veronica shivered. She considered throwing a full tantrum, with stomping and bawling, but then, sensing that she had pushed her mother's patience close to the limit, she quit complaining and ran off dramatically.

A few days later, sidling into the school gym for dress rehearsal, Veronica felt immense relief to see that everyone else's costume looked as dorky as hers. Peter and the grandfather wore bib overalls, flannel shirts, and straw hats. The hunters wore camo fatigues and battered boots from the Army Surplus store and carried popguns over their shoulders. The cat had whiskers painted across her cheeks and a cap with pointy ears. The bird wasn't too ugly, all in blue with a real tutu from a catalog, but her legs were pudgy and her tiara kept slipping. Even Turk Richards, Veronica had to admit, looked silly in his wolf getup: gray leggings, shorts made from brown fur-cloth, matching furry hat, ruff, and mittens, a tail as shaggy as a dust mop, and enough black greasepaint on his face to transform his mouth and chin into a muzzle.

"Ronnie, you look delicious," he told her.

As though his voice was a wand, Veronica suddenly felt herself changing. The new swellings on her body tingled. Her arms became wings, feathered and strong, and her feet seemed to lift from the gymnasium floor. When the recording of *Peter and the Wolf* began playing, and the oboe announced her theme, she glided forward on Prokofiev's music, panting with excitement, the air in her throat no longer stale with gossip and wisecracks and sweat from school, but the pure atmosphere breathed by stars.

On the night of the performance, the Mills family arrived at the gym early enough to claim seats on the first row of the bleachers. Jeanne and Bruce, worried that other teenagers might think they were interested in a kids' show, lounged at one end looking bored. Next to them Danny sat clunking his shoes against the bleachers while he drew pictures on a sketchpad, then came the two grandmothers chattering away, Papaw Hawkins leaning with both hands on his cane, Mabel keeping watch over everybody, and finally, next to the wall and the drinking fountain, there was Gordon, his face inflamed from the choke hold of the white shirt and tie he wore for weddings and funerals.

"I won't understand a thing," Gordon had told Mabel while she was knotting his tie earlier that evening.

"Sure you will," Mabel had answered. "The principal's going to read the story as the music plays."

"What's Mr. Skateboard mean when he says he gets to eat Veronica up?"

"You'll see. And don't get upset. Everything turns out all right."

Gordon would have felt more at ease if he and the rest of the nattering crowd had been waiting for a basketball game instead of a ballet. The baskets were cranked up to the ceiling, however, and the floor was cluttered with scenery: a miniature barn meant for storing yard tools, a picket fence with a gate, a blue tarp spread over the midcourt line to represent the pond, and a forest of plastic Christmas trees on loan from various attics. Gordon fixed his gaze on the rumpled tarp, for Mabel had told him that's where Veronica would dance.

"When's it going to start?" Papaw Hawkins whispered hoarsely.

"Any time now, Papaw," Mabel answered.

The old man's hands were propped on the cane, his chin rested on the hands, and his eyes were drifting closed.

With a snapping of switches, all the lights went out except for those shining down on center court. The audience hushed, except for Gordon, who only realized he was humming when Mabel reached over and pinched his thigh. With a crackle of loudspeakers, the music began. Now and again it was interrupted by the voice of the principal, Mrs. Bee, for whom Gordon had installed a water heater on a recent Saturday. Mrs. Bee was used to pinning hundreds of kids in their chairs with the weight of her words. Now she laid out the story of *Peter and the Wolf* so clearly that even Gordon could follow.

The characters emerged from the mini-barn, each one announced by a bit of music. Papaw Hawkins fell asleep, the two grandmothers clapped at odd moments, Mabel kept scanning the family for trouble, and Gordon resumed humming under the spell of the catchy tunes.

Well along in the story, the duck took the stage alone, such a graceful creature, and Gordon's heart swelled. Then out from the forest of two-by-fours crept the wolf, eyes squinted, jaws snapping. Gordon clenched his fists.

Mabel patted his knee and murmured, "Don't get worked up, now. It's only a play."

Only a play, Gordon kept repeating to himself. And yet Veronica seemed truly frightened as she scuttled about on the blue tarp of the pond, with the wolf in pursuit. Faster and faster she circled, the bill of her orange hat bobbing askew, her white-gloved hands beating the air, while the wolf kept gaining on her. In another few strides the beast would catch her, clamp its teeth in her throat, drag her down.

Suddenly Gordon was in motion, jerking away from Mabel's grasp, rising from the bleachers, striding across the gym floor. Only when the duck reared up and Veronica's pale face glared at him, appalled, did Gordon realize he had seized the wolf by the shoulders and was shaking the scrawny body until the teeth clacked together, and only then could he hear above the music his daughter shrieking, "No, Daddy! *No no no!*"

Wilderness

*I*n March, the smell of thawing dirt sent a jazzy tremor through Gordon Mills. With the windows on his pickup cranked all the way down for the first time that spring, he was driving home from his graveyard shift at the city garage one morning, as groggy as a bear emerging from hibernation, when he caught an earthy whiff that filled him with longing. His thick hands, callused from grappling with metal all winter, began to dance on the steering wheel, eager to plant seeds.

"I wish we had a bit of green out back," he told Mabel at breakfast.

"How about a lawn, like normal folks?" she replied. "I know we're not normal, but at least we can pretend."

"No, something woodsy," Gordon insisted. "Like a bunch of trees with moss and ferns, maybe a pond with turtles and frogs and briar patches and thickets where critters can hide."

Mabel, who still sighed at Gordon's harebrained schemes even after a quarter century of marriage, gazed out the kitchen window and saw not so much a backyard as a junkyard. Except for the garden plot, which Gordon kept clear for the annual crop of vegetables, every square foot out back was crammed with extinct radios and televisions, lawn mowers in various stages of disassembly, giant spools that once held telephone cable, piles of salvaged lumber, eviscerated appliances, electric motors as large as yearling pigs, odd gears and cogs, along with mystery objects hidden under tarps. The neighbors had shielded themselves from the view with tall wooden fences and satellite dishes massive enough to pick up messages from Mars. For Mabel, the yard was a perennial eyesore. She had long since given up complaining to Gordon about it.

"I'd be amazed if there's so much as a dandelion still alive under all that mess," she said.

"You wait," said Gordon. "As soon as I come home from work Saturday morning, I'll get the kids to help me clean it up. Then we'll bring in some plants from the country, and before you know it, we'll have rabbits and raccoons."

"Flowers and grass and fruit trees I wouldn't mind," said Mabel, "but I can do without the wildlife." After dealing with a pack of headstrong kids and cranky grandparents all day, she had her hands full already with two-legged animals.

Weary of machines that broke and a house that kept falling apart, Gordon reckoned that a patch of woods, once you set it growing, would look after itself. What he had in mind was a miniature version of the woodlot he remembered from his grandparents' farm. He had always lived in town, indeed in the same poky Indiana town, which had swollen during his lifetime into a small city, but as a boy he often visited Mammy and Pappy Mills on their two hundred acres, including forty acres of trees that had never been cut. Rows of corn or soybeans gave way at the edge of the woods to a fringe of wildflowers, then berry bushes, then low colorful trees like redbud and dogwood, then to colonies of ferns and mushrooms and pawpaws, and finally to big shadowy maples and beeches and hickories and oaks. If he sat quietly in the woodlot, before long the birds would begin chittering, squirrels and chipmunks would resume scurrying, and a deer or a fox might mosey by. All these years later, long after his grandparents had died, after the farm had been sold and the trees had been cut down to make way for a drag strip, he swallowed hard whenever he thought of that green and tangled place.

Most mornings following his midnight shift in the city garage, bone tired, he shuffled home and collapsed into bed just as everybody else in the household was getting up. Mabel, the children, and the grandparents tiptoed about and spoke in whispers until he began to snore, after which time he would have slept through a motorcycle rally. On the next Saturday morning, however, keeping to his plan, Gordon rolled home from work in a borrowed dump truck, banged his lunch pail on the kitchen table, rounded up the four kids, and marched into the backyard.

They had to walk single file, like pilgrims, along the narrow paths that wound through the junk. Fortunately, the children had taken after Mabel, who was slender, instead of Gordon, who was broad enough to occupy two-thirds of the marital bed. While he had to squeeze through in places—where the path led between the chassis of a motor scooter and a seized-up cement mixer, for instance—the children passed through with ease.

For Gordon, this hoard of scraps and hulks was a memorial to all the devices that had ever failed him, as well as to years of fixing up his ramshackle house. For the children, the yard was a maze of nooks and crannies, ideal for hiding out. Danny favored a patch of smooth clay that was perfect for playing marbles. Veronica's hideaway was a fairy hut she had fashioned out of shipping pallets. Even Bruce, who had reached the mature altitude of high school, and Jeanne, who was working her way through college, still had their favorite places for curling up when they wished to be alone. For Bruce, it was a spot from which he could view the night sky through his telescope. For Jeanne, it was under a trellis in the garden where she had learned to overcome her fear of vegetables. Now, grumpy over having to do chores on a Saturday morning, one by one the children slipped into their cubbyholes and pretended not to hear when Gordon called.

As he began piling warped lumber on the liftgate at the back of the dump truck, his calls became louder and sterner, and when they reached a certain menacing roar, the children emerged from hiding and set to work. Shuttling back and forth, they carried armload after armload to the truck. When Gordon noticed Bruce passing by carrying a stack of dented hubcaps, he thought how easily those dents could be hammered out, and he nearly asked him to set them aside, and he almost told Jeanne not to pitch the box of leaky hoses that only needed new couplings to be almost as good as new. But no, no— if he began rescuing things, he'd never empty the yard. Better make a clean sweep.

Gordon threw himself into the job, and the children caught his enthusiasm. Whatever was too bulky for lifting, he tore apart with a crowbar, dismantled with wrenches, sliced up with an acetylene torch, or dragged to the truck with a winch. Thus he butchered a riding mower, a doghouse, a telephone booth, a pin-setting mechanism from a bowling alley, and a van that had once served as a chicken coop. All the while, he sang snatches of tunes he had learned from his father, tunes that bumped and looped and repeated themselves without ever finishing. Whiskey tunes, his mother called them, because his father broke into song most often when he'd been drinking.

Now and again, from an open window, one or another of the grandparents called out encouragement. Granny Mills cautioned Gordon not to hurt his back and warned the kids not to cut themselves on rusty junk and get lockjaw and wind up in the hospital. Papaw Hawkins offered to come down and help, then Mamaw Hawkins declared that he would do no such thing, not at his age, not unless he wanted to have a coronary and leave her to live out her days alone.

When Mabel glanced from the kitchen at midmorning, she was amazed to see patches of bare dirt where, for as long as she could remember, there had been nothing but scrap metal and warped lumber.

To the gatekeeper at the county landfill, Gordon Mills was almost as familiar as the crows that picked over the rubbish. In fact, Gordon usually came by, like the crows, to see what he could scrounge. Today, however, instead of gathering trash, he was dumping one truckload after another.

"What's got into you, Mills?" the gatekeeper asked. "How come you to throw out all that useful stuff?"

"I'm cleaning up the yard," Gordon shouted over the rumble of the engine.

"Wife get on your case?"

"Naw, it was my idea."

"And what's the idea?"

"Going to grow a woods."

After surrendering five loads to the dump, the backyard, except for the garden plot, was reduced to a scab of raw clay, about the way Earth must have looked, Gordon imagined, before the first plants crept out of the oceans onto land.

"Not a dandelion," Mabel observed, "not a blade of grass."

"You wait," said Gordon.

The packet of wildflower seeds he bought from the 24-Hour Handy Hardware on Sunday morning advised him to loosen the soil before planting. Having been crushed for years under the weight of junk, however, the red clay resisted the shovel and bent the tines on the tiller. So Gordon recruited the children to gouge the clay with screwdrivers, and he followed after them, scattering seeds.

While Danny stayed behind to water the plantings, the three older children rode into the country with Gordon in the pickup. They drove and drove, past shopping malls, used car lots, warehouses, factories, roller-skating rinks, bowling alleys, limestone mills, suburban mini-ranches, and evangelical churches surrounded by vast parking lots, until they finally came to a patch of woods. There were hand-lettered signs posted along the road, however, declaring KEEP OUT! SECOND AMENDMENT TERRITORY! THIS LAND PROTECTED BY CITI-ZEN FIREPOWER! So Gordon kept driving.

At last they rolled to a stop beside a field of stumps. Here and there orange ribbons fluttered from stakes marking the outlines of yet another subdivision. The soil had been churned raw by bulldozer treads, and the ground lay covered in slash. The assault had occurred so recently that sap still oozed from the stumps.

"Why stop here, Daddy?" Veronica asked. "Everything's dead."

"Maybe not," Gordon said. "The ground's still full of roots and bulbs and seeds. If we dig some clumps and plant them in our yard, who knows what might come up?" So they all piled out and started digging, wielding their shovels gingerly, so as not to disturb whatever might be alive in the dirt, and they soon filled the bed of the pickup.

Back at the house, where Danny had faithfully kept spraying the hose on the wildflower seeds, the stubborn clay of the backyard had been transformed into a succulent bog. What Gordon needed now was some of that warped lumber he had carted off, to lay over the mud for a walkway. Not having any spare boards, he took off his boots and socks, rolled up his jeans, and waded into the quagmire, setting out the salvaged clumps of dirt and squishing them down into the goo.

Altogether, he and the children made three trips to the field of stumps, leaving hundreds of holes to puzzle the developers.

That night before joining Mabel in bed, aching all over, Gordon peered out from the basement window into the backyard. For now, it was a barren smear of mud. But he could imagine wonders sprouting there once the seeds and bulbs and roots awoke from their winter drowse.

Around midnight, roused from sleep by the moans of several children and by his own furious itching, Gordon began to suspect that one of the unknown plants lurking in the mud was poison ivy. As he waited in line behind the children for Mabel to daub him with calamine lotion, he recollected how his father, weepy from whiskey, used to say that if you want roses, you have to put up with thorns.

Over the next few weeks, as green shoots sprouted from the muck, thorns proved to be one of the main crops.

"Blackberry, raspberry, and greenbrier," announced Mamaw Hawkins, who had spent her youth in the country and learned all the local plants in 4-H, with an emphasis on everything dangerous. Over the next couple of months, picking her way through the brambles in boots and a pair of Papaw Hawkins' coveralls, she identified other noxious plants. In addition to poison ivy, poison oak, and poison sumac, there were purplish vines called deadly nightshade, stands of giant hogweed and stinging nettles that would raise blisters on skin, and three kinds of deadly mushrooms, including ones known as destroying angels. If she were the mother and not merely the grandmother of those precious children, Mamaw Hawkins confided to Mabel, she wouldn't let them set foot in the backyard.

"Not that I'm trying to tell you how to raise your kids," Mamaw Hawkins added.

"Of course not," said Mabel. "Perish the thought."

When creamy flowers burst open on the blackberries, they attracted swarms of bees. Blood ticks hid in the bushes, chiggers roosted in the tall grass, and mosquitoes cruised over the stagnant pools, intent on burrowing into the first warm body that happened by. What with bugs and bees and thorns and poisonous plants, there was much in the yard to discourage visitors. Before long, the yard came in to visit the house, in the form of moths that flew in to infest wool sweaters, snakes that slithered through cracks in the foundation and curled up in closets, vines that clamped their suckers onto window screens, field mice that raided cupboards, and pollen that set the entire family sneezing.

"It's green, you'll have to admit," Gordon remarked to Mabel one evening, after she had returned from taking two kids to the doctor for hives.

"I'm having fonder and fonder memories of that junk pile," said Mabel. "Every time I check on Danny and Veronica in bed, I expect to find water moccasins wrapped around their necks."

"We're too far north for water moccasins," Gordon said.

"Copperheads, then."

"Whoever said nature was nice? You can't pick and choose. It's all or nothing."

"One more nuisance from that thicket," Mabel said, "and I'll vote for nothing."

Supper that evening was accompanied by hooting from the back lot, a sound quickly identified by Veronica as the call of a barred owl, for she had memorized the voices of every bird native to southern Indiana. Now she reproduced the sound so persuasively that the owl hooted back. The two carried on a dialogue for several minutes, ceasing only when Veronica shoveled a forkful of spaghetti into her mouth. Amid the silence that followed, the family seated around the table heard a high-pitched howling that set all their spines tingling.

"Coyotes," Danny whispered, eyes round with delight.

"He takes after you," Mabel complained to Gordon. "If men could get pregnant, they wouldn't be such fans of nature."

On a morning not long after the coyote serenade, the family awoke to the sound of grunting and snuffling and looked outside to discover a bear in the yard feeding on blackberries. Shouting "Grizzly, grizzly!"

the children came rushing down into Mabel and Gordon's bedroom, where they were soon joined by the grandparents.

Last to arrive, limping carefully down the basement stairs clinging to the banister, was Mamaw Hawkins, who squinted out the window and announced reassuringly, "It's not a grizzly, my dears, but an eastern black bear. *Ursus americanus.* They're much less likely to eat you."

Mabel was not reassured. "This has gone too far," she said to Gordon. "Next it will be wolves and cougars."

Danny climbed up on a chair to get a better view from the window. "Wow," he said. "It's bigger than Pops."

Nine sets of eyes peered out at the bear, which grazed on the blackberries with the nearsighted diligence of Papaw Hawkins checking box scores in the sports pages.

Gordon had never come across a bear in his grandparents' woodlot, never a wolf or an eagle, but he had always hoped to meet some creature so fearless it would look back at him with more curiosity than caution. "What's it hurting?" he asked Mabel.

"My nerves," she replied, a confession that was rare enough, coming from Mabel, to stifle any more questions from Gordon. He crept upstairs to the kitchen, eased open the back door, and started banging pots. The bear grazed on indifferently. Gordon ran the electric mixer at top speed, turned on the blender, the vacuum cleaner, every noisy appliance for which he was still paying monthly notes, and all to no effect. So he grabbed a broom and stepped outside, unsure what to do next, when he heard Veronica calling from an upstairs window in a voice that sounded remarkably like the snorting of the bear.

Still munching, the bear swiveled its muzzle up toward the girl, drew its lips back to expose berry-stained teeth, snuffled amiably, and then ambled away. It paused to scratch its back against a corner of the garage, knocking off a section of siding, and then waddled out through a gap in the fence. A fresh gap in the fence, Gordon noted, adding this item along with the garage siding to his mental repair list.

"Sweetheart, listen," Mabel said when she came outside to join him, "I've got more than enough to do keeping nine people fed and clothed and doctored and pacified. I can't take on bears and coyotes and poison mushrooms and snakes. Could we just have flowers and veggies?"

Gordon put up no argument, even though what he saw from the back stoop was beginning to look as green and tangled and inviting as the woods on his grandparents' farm. He borrowed the dump truck again, along with a backhoe, and set about digging up every last sapling and bramble and bush, until the yard was reduced again to a scab of clay. Three of the children helped, but Veronica wouldn't come out of her room, she was so mopey over the loss. When asked what she had said to the bear in its own language, she only shook her head.

Instead of dumping everything back in the field of stumps, which would soon be scoured by earthmovers, Gordon drove until he found an abandoned pasture that was beginning to bristle with young trees, and there he scattered the load by jostling the bed of the truck as he rolled forward. Then he took a shovel and carefully settled each plant into its own pocket of dirt. When he had finished, he straightened up to ease the ache in his back and surveyed the pasture. If left in peace, it would grow into a woodlot, and one day he could bring Veronica here and they could sit quietly together, listening to the critters and trees.

Snow

*E*arly on the Fourth of July, before anyone else in the house was stirring, Gordon lowered himself with a grunt onto a paint-speckled drop cloth on the floor of the garage, opened his glossy new copy of *Yoga for Skeptics*, and tried twisting himself into the poses of the wiry young woman pictured in the book. Neither wiry nor young—just turned fifty, in fact, and built like a retired heavyweight wrestler—Gordon could not begin to wrench his body into those pretzel shapes.

His children had given him the book on his birthday a week earlier, the four of them agreeing, in a rare stroke of unanimity, that yoga was just the tonic needed by a father turning half a century old.

"We thought it might ease your gimpy back, Pops," said Bruce.

"Limber you up," said Danny.

"And let's face it, Daddy," Veronica observed, "you could stand to drop a few pounds."

"Not that we don't adore every ounce of you," put in Jeanne, always the diplomat.

Gordon had to admit he was going to pot. In recent years, his body had come to feel stiff and heavy, as if he were stuffed with sand, and his joints crackled whenever he got up out of a chair. It didn't help that nowadays, what with budget cuts and a hiring freeze, the city had him driving trucks instead of fixing them—garbage trucks, dump trucks, delivery vans, snowplows. Sit eight hours a day on a cushy seat with a cooler of food beside you, and your butt will spread like warm butter. The widest men he'd ever seen were those who rode all day in a police cruiser or in the cab of a long-haul semi. The men who ran the derricks in the limestone quarries where his father used to work were so broad in the beam, they had to get their overalls custom made from army surplus tents, according to the old man.

Gordon could have slept in on the Fourth of July because the parade didn't start until noon, and his only assignment was to clean up the streets afterward with the sweeper truck. Instead, he rose at the crack of dawn, as he had been doing each morning since his birthday, plodded to the garage, and spent a furtive half hour stretching and groaning. He reminded himself that he was doing this for the sake of his family, who needed him to keep his old ticker ticking, yet he didn't want his kids or wife or the grandparents watching him while he struggled to mimic the poses of the sleek young woman. "The postures of yoga represent the ideal shapes that are hidden inside you," the book assured him. The shapes must have been hidden mighty deep, Gordon figured, because he hadn't come within shouting distance of them so far.

Although the garage was already turning into an oven from the July heat, he didn't open the door for fear that an early dog walker might spy him there in his horseshoe-spangled Indianapolis Colts boxer shorts, lathered in sweat. And thus he was caught by surprise in one of the more painful yoga positions when the overhead door began to rise on its track, and all four kids came bursting in to announce that a blizzard had swept in overnight and buried the city in two feet of snow.

Wise to their jokes, Gordon relaxed his corkscrewed body and sat up, preparing to give them the laugh they expected, but he closed his mouth before he made a sound, because, sure enough, a white drift filled the mouth of the garage and a blanket of snow covered everything as far as he could see. While Danny and Veronica, still in their pajamas, danced along the edge of the drift, and Bruce and Jeanne approached the snow cautiously on bare feet, Gordon pawed through the laundry basket until he found a grimy pair of coveralls to put on. Wouldn't you know it, on his morning off he would have to drive the plow. Well, at least the storm should cool things off.

"Holy cow, it's warm!" shouted Danny. He wriggled his fingers in the drift and threw handfuls into the air. With degrees of skepticism proportional to their ages, the other children did the same, each in turn crying with amazement and delight, even Jeanne, the college sophisticate, who prided herself on having put away childish things. Soon all four of them waded into the driveway, whooping and hollering.

Gordon shuffled over and poked a hand into the wall of snow. It wasn't so much warm as a kind of no-temperature, dry and feathery like corn flakes or confetti. Warm or cold, why did it have to snow on his morning off? The pickup and minivan, parked on the drive so as to leave room in the garage for his yoga, were two gleaming humps. A thick frosting coated everything—houses across the way, bushes and trees, mailboxes, telephone poles, satellite dishes, fire hydrants. The street, untraveled so far on this holiday morning, curved away as white and smooth as a bathtub. Not a breeze moved. Not a bird sang. Not a motor revved. The world might have seemed fixed and final, if the kids hadn't been sliding down the hood of the truck on the seats of their pajamas, shouting like pirates.

None of them offered to help shovel, nor did Gordon have the heart to ask them, they were so stoked with joy. He fetched the grain scoop from its hook in the garage and started clearing a path to the front door. At least it was light, this July snow. Lucky thing, since the yoga had only made his gimpy back gimpier. When he threw a shovelful over his shoulder, the white flakes giddied and floated like the downy seeds of dandeli-ons. Still, no matter how light, no matter how warm, two feet of snow was two feet of snow. Long before he reached the front door, he was sweating like a mule, his heart was thumping, and his back was twitching.

"Yoga will liberate your spine," Jeanne had assured him on his birth-day. "It will fire up your chakras, align your energy flow, and reveal your ageless self beneath the illusion of flesh."

Right now, as he shoveled, his flesh felt pretty convincing. Far from loosening him, the exercises had made him feel like a snarled knot, the kind that gets tighter the more you work to loosen it. He leaned for a moment on the grain scoop to let his ticker slow down, reflecting that if he really had an ageless self tucked away somewhere inside, now would be a good time for it to show up and give his aging self a break.

Just then a window clunked open and a voice called out, "Gordon, there's been a blizzard!" and a second voice cried, "You foolish man, you'll catch your death of cold!" and a third voice hollered, "Come indoors this minute and get some clothes on!" In this way, Gordon learned that all three grandparents were up. He went back to digging.

Presently the kitchen window opened, and Mabel shouted, "The su-pervisor's on the phone and says to report for snowplow duty pronto. But I say you eat breakfast first."

Outnumbered as usual, Gordon allowed Mabel to stuff him with oatmeal and banana and wheat germ and skimmed milk and English muffins while she packed his lunch pail, and then, to humor the grand-parents, he bundled up in winter clothes, from boots to knitted cap. As he trudged past the buried van and pickup, where his children had been joined by neighbor kids, all squealing and sliding, Gordon real-ized there was no way he could drive to work. So he waved goodbye to his family and waded through the snow toward the city equipment yard, lunch pail clunking against his leg.

As soon as he passed beyond sight of the house, he took off the hat, gloves, scarf, coat, and flannel shirt, carrying them along in a bundle.

Still he sweated, and the flakes stuck to him like feathers in a pil-low fight. When he finally reached the lot where the snowplows were parked, he could tell from the unmarked drifts that he was the first to arrive. No sooner had he climbed into his truck and started the engine than voices began to fire instructions from the radio.

"All available plows report immediately to the mayor's house . . . to police headquarters . . . to station WXTZ . . . to Our Lady of the Highways Hospital . . . to the Perpetual American Bank . . . to Stone Country Bowl-ing Lanes . . . ."

Gordon tried hard to fulfill all of these errands, zigzagging across the city in his parrot-green truck with the scooped blade in front and the swiveling red light on top and the yellow hazard lights blinking in back. But no sooner did he set off toward one destination than he was called in three other directions. He drove as fast as he dared. The snow flew away before him, airy as goose down. In the rearview mirror he could see it settling again in his wake. He imagined himself piloting an icebreaker, plowing the polar seas, with the icepack closing behind. Twice he drove by his own house, honking at the mob of kids, and on the second pass he found the snow as deep as ever.

Soon other green trucks were on the roads, driven by guys from the maintenance crew, but they might as well have been plowing water, for all the good they were doing. Unable to clear the streets, Gordon began picking up riders, ferrying them to places they needed to reach. Thus he carried three civil defense wardens to fire stations, two soldiers to the bus depot (from which, he reckoned, no buses would be leaving), a doc-tor to a woman in labor, two girls to a volleyball tournament, a couple of grandparents to a birthday party, a painter to her studio, and a harpsi-cord player to his harpsicord. The passengers could see that Gordon was busy handling the truck, so they limited themselves to brief remarks on the order of "Crazy weather, hey?" or "If you ask me, it's a sign."

With help from the passengers, Gordon's lunch pail was empty be-fore midmorning, even though Mabel had packed it to the brim. By that hour, it was so hot in the truck that Gordon had to leave the windows open, with apologies to the riders, for the snow blew in and settled on everyone in the cab, like a bleached version of the fluff that gathers under beds—widow's wool, his mother called it.

The more plows joined him on the streets, the denser the whirl of flakes in the air, as though the city were being shaken inside one of those clear little globes with a winter scene inside. Snow blurred the truck's windshield faster than the wipers could scrape it clean. The white haze separated Gordon from the world, creating a screen on which he saw not only the young woman tied in yoga postures, but also jugglers, gymnasts, trampoline artists, guitarists running their fingers lightning fast over the frets, tennis players leaping to return shots, circus acrobats doing flips in the air, lovers coupling in ways never before attempted.

Forget it, Gordon told himself. You're not cut out for such moves.

He kept driving.

Toward noon, when the marchers were lining up for the July Fourth parade, more snow began to fall, great lacy flakes that dawdled and swerved on their way down, as though from the plucking of a skyful of chickens. The start of the parade was delayed until Gordon could pull up in front to clear a path, and so it happened that his snowplow led the way, followed by strutting high school bands, leaping cheerleaders in short skirts, veterans in faded uniforms, politicians with gleaming teeth, six-legged dragons, jugglers, and clowns, cops in squad cars, firefighters on hook-and-ladder trucks, farmers on tractors, Shriners on miniature motorcycles, queens in sundresses and kings in shirts paler than powdered sugar.

Hunched over the steering wheel, peering into the blizzard, Gordon pictured the city as God might see it—the courthouse square, the grid of streets, the patchwork of parks, the snaky river, the sprawling suburbs, all blanketed in snow—and flowing through the whiteness a stream of brilliant colors, a parade of people and their gaudy machines following a parrot-green truck, and inside the truck a driver carefully steering, and inside the driver a dimly burning light.

Dinosaur

At fifty, Gordon could just barely remember what it had felt like, as a kid, to shut his eyes at bedtime and open them again, seemingly an instant later, with sunlight streaming through the curtains, and then to spring out of bed without a single ache. Now he dreaded the nights, which were broken up by fretful dreams and bodily gripes, and he dreaded the mornings, when every joint and limb complained.

"Compared to me, you're a spring chicken," his mother reminded him when he groused about getting old. "There's no use squawking until you've been plucked and thrown in the stew pot."

Gordon's father had never reached fifty, dying early in his forties from booze or bad luck or criminal negligence, depending on who was telling the story. A lawyer had secured a tiny pension for the widowed Granny Mills by arguing that the owners of the quarry where Gordon's father died had been negligent for allowing a drunken man to work. Gordon chalked up the death to bad luck, since his father had fallen asleep in a shady spot where a derrick happened to be setting down a block of limestone the size of a mail truck. Granny Mills insisted that her late husband wouldn't have dozed on the job if he hadn't been possessed, as usual, by the demon drink.

Still, she cashed her pension checks, taking half the amount in quarters, which she carried home from the credit union in a plastic pail. The pail rested beside her on the front seat of her venerable fire-engine-red Pontiac when she drove to the casino in French Lick, where, avoiding the newfangled slot machines that took only credit cards, she fed quarters into the few antique slots that still accepted coins. The pail was usually empty when she drove home. Her rare winnings she set aside to pay for speeding tickets, for in spite of her birdlike frame, she pressed a heavy foot on the gas pedal. She insisted that the smokies merely assumed she must be speeding because she drove a red car.

Granny Mills thought of her gambling jaunts as compensation for having been widowed at forty-three. True, she had been courted in her widowhood by various beaus, all of them sworn to sobriety, but none had claimed her heart the way her frolicsome, handsome, whiskey-guzzling husband had. Three of the beaus had proposed marriage, one of them as recently as her seventy-fifth birthday, but she was not about to begin training another man this late in life. Besides, she had Gordon. He missed out on his father's good looks, dancing feet, and frisky humor, but he inherited a knack with tools and machines, a love of animals and children, and a penchant for kindness. In a mean world, she judged, kindness made up for a lot of shortcomings.

Gordon's shortcomings were frequently pointed out not only by his mother, who did not believe in bottling up her opinions, but also by all of his children except Danny. The boy's leniency may have been due to his youth, since at seven years old he had not yet come under the spell of sports heroes or movie stars or social media celebrities who made Gordon appear, by comparison, clumsy, backward, dimwitted, and dull.

The older children sometimes referred to Gordon as Dinosaur Dad, by way of noting how far behind the times he was, but Danny treated the label as a compliment, for he had read every book in the kids' section of the library on dinosaurs and considered them to be the coolest creatures ever to walk the land or swim the seas. On his side of the attic bedroom he shared with his big brother, the walls were covered with posters of extinct reptiles and the shelves were thronged by models of tyrannosauruses and brontosauruses and a dozen other kinds of lumbering beasts. In the middle of a conversation about birds, Danny was liable to bring up pterodactyls. Mention the summer heat or winter cold, and he would inform you that stegosaurs used the spiky plates along their spines to regulate their temperature. After outgrowing his tricycle, which he called Triceratops, he graduated to a bicycle, which he called Velociraptor. "Like in rapid velocity, you get it?" he would say to anyone who puzzled over the name. Dinosaurs went extinct, Danny explained, not because they were dimwitted, but because they starved and froze after a meteor hit the earth and spewed up clouds of dust that blocked sunlight for years.

Gordon often felt as if his world had been struck by a whole slew of meteors, only these came from laboratories instead of outer space. Engineers were wiping out the jobs that used to be done by guys like him. Nowadays, a strong arm and a stout back no longer counted for much. Any pipsqueak could push buttons. Used to be, you needed strength and skill to run a big machine, like a dozer or a backhoe. Now even women could drive earthmovers, and scrawny guys could run steamrollers. It wouldn't be long before machines were running themselves. According to the TV, pretty soon big rigs would be cruising highways without a human on board, and tractors plowing the fields would be guided by satellites. There were robots that could build other robots, and the ones they built could do the same, on and on, until they covered the whole planet with their offspring. And robots didn't have to daydream or take a leak or stay home sick; they could work twenty-four hours a day, doing anything a laboring man could do, only faster and cheaper. Gordon could foresee a day when a factory would be run by one egghead in a cubicle jabbing at a screen with his index finger. Or maybe just *talking* to the screen, telling it what to do. How long before the screens started jabbering to each other and cut out the egghead? Sooner or later, even brainy guys, and not just brawny ones, would be dinosaurs.

Used to be, working at the city maintenance garage, Gordon could poke around inside a cranky machine, figure out which parts were broken or which gears were out of whack, and set everything right with pliers and screwdrivers and wrenches. Nowadays, half the machines didn't even have gears or other moving parts, just circuit boards plastered with chips, and when one of those boards gave out, you couldn't fix it; you had to throw it out and order a new one from Taiwan or Timbuktu or wherever the infernal things were made. Anymore, to fix a diesel engine, you couldn't just listen to it grumble and growl and then tinker until it purred; you had to hook it up to a computer, which doped out the problem and told you what to do. How long before the computer just went ahead and made the repair without any need for a mechanic?

At least a man could still push a broom, Gordon thought, as he showed up for the graveyard shift one night. No sooner had he clocked in than the supervisor hollered for him to come have a look at the new janitor they were trying out. Wondering what had become of the old janitor, a toothless guy with six kids, Gordon entered the garage, where a silvery wheeled contraption, about the size and shape of a beer keg, was creeping back and forth across the floor, scouring the oil-stained concrete with spinning brushes. As it moved, a domed lid on top swiveled around, shining a red laser like the swinging beam from a lighthouse. When the rolling keg approached an obstacle, such as a tool cart or wheelbarrow, it would stop, blink the red light, and then change direction, never bumping a thing.

"She's called RoboMaid," the supervisor said. "Nifty, eh? And get a load of this." He stuck a leg in front of the machine, which nudged his boot before it could halt.

"Excuse me!" the robot sang out in a girly voice, then quickly backed away.

"Don't let it happen again," the supervisor said.

"Yes, sir!" The robot blinked its laser, swerved around him, and resumed its work.

"You see that, Mills?" the supervisor said. "The first polite employee in the history of the city maintenance department. No complaints, no excuses. No smoke breaks, lunch breaks, or vacations."

With each pass over the floor, the robot left a clean, damp strip, which made the concrete look as if it had been freshly poured. Watching the gadget hum along, Gordon asked about the old janitor, the one with six kids to feed.

"We transferred him to the grounds crew. He can hang on there until the RoboMowers arrive."

"Then what?"

"Then . . . I don't know . . . maybe we can get him retrained."

"To do what?"

The supervisor frowned. "I'm running a garage, Mills, not a charity. Until we can replace the rest of our ancient machines, you've still got work. Why don't you go do it?"

Every machine in the Mills household was ancient, a fact that had once bothered Gordon but now reassured him. When his mother collected a third speeding ticket on her way home from the French Lick Casino, for example, he was able to install a governor on the old Pontiac, which kept her from going over fifty-five. She complained that the car had lost its pep, and Gordon, low on pep himself, promised to see what he could do. Better tell her a white lie than let her keep hot-rodding. If she could have lost her license by getting one more ticket, that would have been fine with Gordon, but he couldn't risk having her crash before the troopers caught her again. Short of losing her license, though, what else would make her quit driving? Whenever Gordon suggested it might be time for her to hand over the keys, she accused him of wanting to pluck her last feathers and throw her in the stew pot.

As if the household's other old machines had decided to gang up on him, one Saturday in August the washer overflowed and flooded the basement, the garbage disposal clogged up, the ceiling fan in the boys' bedroom conked out, and the shower faucet sprang a leak. Late that afternoon, Gordon had just finished repairing the last of these items and was putting his tools away in the garage when Danny sidled up to him pushing his bicycle and announced that Velociraptor had a flat tire.

"Well," said Gordon, summoning up the last of his pep, "we can't have your dinosaur limping around on one tire, now, can we?"

Each of the seven steps Gordon worked through to mend the punctured tube he explained to Danny, who watched closely, taking it all in, just the way Gordon as a boy had watched his own father work. When the wheel was remounted and the tire inflated, Danny took a test ride on the driveway, while Gordon washed up. No matter how hard he scrubbed, grime still showed in the seams of his knuckles and palms, and the food he touched always tasted faintly of oil.

Well before dawn the next morning, a Sunday, with Mabel quietly snoring in bed beside him, Gordon opened his eyes, sensing a presence near him in the darkness. Instead of imagining a burglar or a ghost, he imagined a child, wakened by nightmare or fever or croup.

"Pops," came Danny's whisper from inches away. "Can we go to the park?"

Gordon squinted at the clock. 3:37. The window high in the wall of the basement bedroom was still as black as a crow's wing. "It's a bit early, kiddo," he muttered.

"It's just the right time."

"For what?"

"For meteors."

Fearing their whispers would rouse Mabel, Gordon peeled away the sheet, damp from August humidity, and slid from bed, hitched up his boxer shorts and straightened the kink in his back. Then he reached out until he felt Danny's shoulder, and led the boy upstairs to the kitchen, where they found Granny Mills seated at the table, counting quarters into her plastic pail.

"I'll have you know," she said cheerfully, "last night I won nearly half as much as I lost."

"Did you get caught speeding?" Gordon asked.

"How could I, in that poky old jalopy?" She put on a peeved look, but the sight of Danny made her brighten. "And what gets you up and dressed at this hour, my young man?"

"The Perseid meteor shower," Danny answered. "Dad and I are going to the park to watch." He went on to recount everything he had learned about this celestial event from the latest issue of *Astronomy for Kids*.

Granny Mills pretended to follow his every word, although she could make neither heads nor tails of the business about orbits and radiant points and comet debris. Meanwhile, Gordon rummaged through a basket of laundry on the kitchen floor until he found a pair of jeans to pull on over his boxers and a T-shirt to cover his hairy chest.

When Danny had run out of information, or at least out of breath, Granny Mills broke in to say, "Well, you two should come home clean as a whistle after sitting through a meteor shower."

"It's not that kind of shower, Granny."

Before she could explain that she was teasing, Danny grabbed Gordon's hand and hustled him out the door. They walked the few blocks to the park through air thick enough to spread on toast, yet the sky, speckled with stars, was as clear as a muggy summer night in Indiana could ever be. Danny led them to a grassy hill near the center of the park, far from trees and streetlights, and they lay down there, side by side, still holding hands, on a north-facing slope.

"Where do we look?" Gordon asked.

"Straight up, I think," Danny replied. "Or maybe down a bit."

"And what are we looking for?"

"Shooting stars. Well, not stars, really. They're streaks of comet dust. In pictures they look like straight lines."

Gordon squinted, wanting to see a meteor for his son's sake. But he saw no streaks, no patterns, only a confusion of lights that might have been a mob of fireflies hovering up there. To think that every one of those pinpricks of light was another sun made him dizzy. Earth was home to more marvels than he could take in.

They lay for a while without speaking, the smell of grass and hot soil enveloping them, crickets and cicadas sawing away, and then Danny asked, "Is Granny going to die soon?"

"Not too soon, I hope."

After another silence, Danny squeezed Gordon's hand and cried out, "There's one!"

"Where?"

"Aw, it's gone. Fast as lightning!"

Gordon stared without blinking, not wanting to miss the next meteor. But Danny spotted another and another before Gordon finally saw a streak of light. "Wow," he murmured, running a thumb over the back of his son's trembling hand.

During the next hour or so they spied dozens more. Gordon couldn't help remembering rocket fire lighting up the sky over the airstrip in Saudi Arabia as he leveled the sand with a grader. He could have died in that desert. Some of his buddies did. But he had survived, and if little else had come of his life, he had helped make this child, and three other children who were asleep back in the house, a house dry and safe and stocked with food.

Finally, as the eastern sky began to lighten and the stars dimmed, Danny asked, "Do you think maybe scientists will bring back the dinosaurs one day? You know, make new ones in the lab from fossil poop or something?"

"Could be," Gordon said. "You never can tell what scientists might do."

"I hope they start with Tyrannosaurus rex and put one right here in the park."

"That would liven things up, for sure."

"I guess they'd have to put it in a cage, or else it would eat people."

"A cage would be a good idea."

Danny frowned, putting a crease in his smooth forehead. "If a big meteor hit the earth, do you think we'd all starve and freeze?'

"Oh," Gordon answered, "we'd figure out some way to keep going."

They exchanged no more words for a dozen heartbeats. Robins and sparrows began cranking up their morning songs as the crickets and cicadas quieted down. Dogs barked. A siren wailed from the hospital and then tapered away as the ambulance ran its errand.

Then Danny released a puff of air, as if someone had punched him in the belly. In a hushed voice, he said, "You and Mom are going to die someday, aren't you?"

Gordon thought how to answer, knowing he could die tomorrow. He could die on the way home from the park. Eyes burning, he decided to opt for hope. "Someday, but a long, long time from now. We want to stick around to watch you grow up and maybe meet your kids, if you have kids."

"That's funny to think of. Me, a dad." Laughing, and letting go of Gordon's hand, Danny rolled down the slope.

Gordon struggled to his feet, every joint rebelling. As he rubbed his back and flexed his knees, he watched his boy race back up the hill, the young face, free of scars and worry lines, shining in the first light.

Anniversary

*G*ordon vividly recalled the sultry summer day of his wedding—
the churring of cicadas and the smell of new-mown grass
when he stepped outdoors that morning, the sweat stinging
his eyes as he drove to the UU church, the borrowed necktie strangling him as he stood waiting beside the minister in front of more eyes
watching him than at any moment since his last high school wrestling
match, and then, oh glory, Mabel gliding down the aisle, holding on to
her dad by the crook of his elbow, as if to keep from floating into the air,
a grin on her face as wide as sunrise, while her mom and his mom and
half the other women in the crowd smiled and cried at the same time,
then the lady minister pouring all kinds of blessings over them before
declaring them husband and wife, and everybody clapping when he
and his brand-new bride kissed, then birdseed raining down on them
as they left the church and climbed into his pickup, the rattle of stones
in the hubcaps as they pulled away—those, and a hundred other details
from his wedding day he recalled with ease; but he could not for the life
of him remember the date.

Which is why he kept a yellowing slip of paper marked JUNE 25
on the pegboard over his workbench in the garage. The paper was

yellowing because it had been reminding him of the date for twenty-four years. As June rolled around each year, he thought of anniversary presents he might buy for Mabel, the sorts of things she wouldn't buy for herself—like peach perfume or a lace nightie or rabbit-fur slippers—but he never actually bought anything. It wasn't so much the expense that held him back, since he could have scrounged up the cash, as it was his dread of shopping, which rivaled his dread of computers and phones. He didn't mind going to the hardware store or lumberyard, where he knew his way around; he could hustle in, find the items he needed, pay without using a credit card, and then hustle back out and drive home to tackle whatever jobs were waiting. But the prospect of entering a shopping mall, let alone a ladies' clothing store, made him shiver. Once, looking for a bag of composted cow manure in one of those giant box stores that sells everything under the sun, he had stumbled into the lingerie department, where the sight of female mannequins dressed in underwear made him turn around and flee.

And so, because he was allergic to shopping, and a tightwad to boot, Gordon always made anniversary presents for Mabel with his own hands. Of the twenty-four gifts he had made so far, the very first remained one of his favorites. It was a necklace of copper washers bent into birdlike shapes and strung on the pull chain from a ceiling fan. All these years later, it still dangled from a spindle on Mabel's jewelry cabinet, which he had made for the second anniversary, and she still wore it on special occasions. More than once, in those early years, she had greeted him in bed wearing nothing but that necklace.

So far as possible, he made the anniversary presents with materials he had scavenged here and there, thus avoiding trips to the store. When the old high school was torn down, he salvaged a section of the bleachers and used the seasoned pine to make a stepstool for the kitchen one year, a spice rack another year, and a picnic table a third year. With a load of bricks he'd picked up from the ruins of a housefire, he laid out a patio for one anniversary and built a barbecue pit for the next. He used scraps of leftover plywood to build a mailbox shaped like a barn, a miniature replica of the one he remembered from his grandparents' farm. For several anniversaries, he used stuff rescued from the dump to make yard ornaments, which Mabel asked him to display in back of the house, where the family could admire them in private. With other finds from the dump, he rigged a trellis to hold a crop of sugar snap peas and cucumbers, a fence to keep deer out of the garden, and a satellite dish that picked up old movies for free.

The one anniversary present he could never come up with, no matter how hard he tried, was finding a way to keep the basement dry. He didn't mind stepping into a puddle when he got out of bed on a night of heavy rain, but it galled him that Mabel had to slog through water to visit the bathroom on such a night or to reach the stairway in the morning. He had tried every remedy in the books, and a few that had never made it into the books, but none of them did the trick.

Brooding about the swampy basement reminded him of the year he surprised Mabel on their anniversary with the sculpture of an alligator he'd carved with his chainsaw from the trunk of a lightning-killed sweetgum tree and how amazed she was by the way he'd whittled every detail, from the bumps on the hide to the sharp teeth. This memory lifted his mood a bit and set loose another watery recollection, of the time he helped volunteers from the local land trust lay out a board-walk through a wetland where eagles and herons nested, and by troll-ing around in his head like this he suddenly thought of just the right present for their twenty-fifth anniversary, a sure way to keep Mabel's feet dry in the basement even if it rained cats and dogs and polliwogs. He would build a boardwalk, only instead of leading past the nests of herons and eagles, it would lead from Mabel's side of the bed to the bathroom and on beyond to the base of the stairs. He calculated that he had enough varnished pine left from the old high school bleachers to provide the decking, enough treated two-by-fours to serve as string-ers, and enough carpet remnants to cover the planks so her bare feet wouldn't get cold. This idea set him humming, and on the first weekend in June he set to work.

Whenever Gordon emerged from the garage that first weekend in June, Mabel noticed he was humming one of his ragged little tunes with more gusto than usual, and even with a hint of melody, and whenever he passed within kissing distance of her he paused to deliver a smooch. Given the time of year, she took the frequent nuzzling and boisterous humming as signs that he was at work on a present for their anniversary, which meant the garage would be off-limits to her from now until the twenty-fifth.

Gordon liked to surprise her with his homemade gifts, and some were quite surprising—such as the crow he had stuffed after it flew into the cab of his garbage truck at the dump one day and died right there on the seat beside him or the tin cans he had mashed flat and soldered into the shape of a tepee big enough for her to crawl inside—but most of the gifts were useful, such as the potholders sewn from the leather of retired welder's gloves or the grape arbor lashed together from the handles of worn-out brooms. Whether useful or weird, all of the anniversary presents were endearing, simply because Gordon had dreamed them up and had fashioned them with his thick-fingered, callused, curiously deft hands.

Thinking of those hands, Mabel remembered how tenderly they had roamed her body that night after the wedding, as she lay beside him atop their joined sleeping bags on the shore of Lake Debs in the Hoosier National Forest. A brisk wind kept mosquitos at bay and ruffled up waves that glinted in the starlight. The night was warm enough for them to leave their clothes in the tent, and clear enough to reveal the Milky Way. Gordon told her the names of constellations and a few of the brightest stars, but as he slowly ran his fingers over her skin she forgot all of the names, except for those of the two visible planets, Venus and Jupiter. He had learned to read the night sky while camping as a boy on his grandparents' farm, but she had never slept outside before, let alone done so naked with a man at her side. The weight of his big hand, so tender, so calm, reassured her. She lost track of time, but they stayed there under the stars long enough for Venus to disappear below the western horizon and for mosquitos to force them back inside the tent.

Their honeymoon lasted one full day, from the moment they pulled out of the church parking lot with birdseed in their hair, and the stones Gordon's buddies had put inside the hubcaps clattering away, until Sunday afternoon, when they had to break camp and return to town so they could go to their jobs on Monday. Gordon had just begun working at the city maintenance garage, so he wasn't eligible for vacation yet; and Mabel was relatively new in her own job of connecting local farmers to the food pantry, community kitchen, and restaurants, so she couldn't take time off either, especially in June, with so many crops ready for harvest.

Those memories were so fresh in her mind, she could hardly believe that twenty-five years had passed since their wedding, but the calendar told her it was so, and the passage of time was confirmed by her reflection in the mirror and by the sounds of four children and three grandparents and one husband stirring here and there throughout the house, eight beloved and sometimes vexing souls, each of whom would soon be needing something that only she could provide.

In a rare break from her duties that first weekend in June, Mabel sat down on the back porch to share a pot of peppermint tea with Jeanne, who clearly had a bee in her bonnet. As the oldest of the Mills children, Jeanne was the first to become curious about the lives her parents had led before her birth, especially their courtship and the early days of their marriage, and so she was the first to learn that their honeymoon had lasted only a single day.

"But it was a delicious day," Mabel remarked when Jeanne chastened her for describing a one-night stand in a tent as a honeymoon. "And we didn't do much standing," Mabel added with a reminiscent smile.

"Mom, *really*." Jeanne bent over her mug of tea as if to inhale the minty aroma, but actually to hide her blush.

Mabel laughed. "Do you think you arrived by way of immaculate conception?"

"Well, you didn't conceive me on your wedding night, that's for sure. I've always wondered why you waited six years to have your first baby."

"We didn't wait."

"You couldn't get pregnant?"

"I got pregnant twice, and each time we shared the news with family and friends, the way young couples do, but then I had two miscarriages. It took me a long while after each loss before I was willing to risk another one."

Jeanne studied her mother's face, trying to imagine what it would feel like to carry a new life in your womb and then lose it. "I'm so sorry," she murmured.

"Oh, you made up for it, sweetie. You and Bruce and Veronica and Danny."

Sensing the moment was ripe for airing an idea she had been hatching for weeks, Jeanne said, "You and Dad should do something special this year to mark a quarter century of marriage."

"A quarter century! Now you're making me feel ancient. That sounds so much longer than twenty-five years."

"However you measure it, for characters like you and Dad to stay married that long is amazing. You should celebrate. When Dad gets his vacation in August, why don't you two go off by yourselves for a week and finally have a real honeymoon?"

"Go away for a week? I can't possibly do that."

"Why not?"

"There's so much that needs to be done."

"So tell me, and I'll make a list."

"To begin with, what will you eat?"

"We all know how to cook, thanks to your teaching. Even Danny can make chocolate chip cookies. And the grannies will make sure we don't starve."

"But there's Danny soccer . . ."

"His games end in July. I checked."

"What about your summer classes?"

"They're all online."

And so it went for half an hour, Mabel coming up with reasons why she couldn't leave the house for a week—Bruce's driving lessons, the skateboard boy lurking around Veronica, Papaw's bad heart, Mamaw's gimpy hip, Granny's confusion, the vegetable garden, property taxes coming due—and Jeanne kept swatting aside every excuse, finally saying, with an exasperated air, "Mom, you've just got to let go."

Mabel sighed, unable to explain why she resisted Jeanne's proposal. There was the cost, of course, always a constraint in their low-budget household; and there was Gordon's list of things he needed to build or fix during his two-week vacation; but her chief reason for resisting, she realized, was that she thought of herself as irreplaceable—the only person who knew the location of every item in the house, who carried a hundred recipes in her head, who kept track of all the food in the pantry and all the clothes in the closets and every bill awaiting payment, who remembered birthdays and bought presents, who looked in on neighbors and maintained contact with far-flung relatives, who managed the calendar and checkbook and doctors' appointments, who consoled and advised and cheered up and nursed children and grandparents and husband, any time of day or night, and who never, ever, abandoned her post at the heart of the family.

As if reading her thoughts, Jeanne said, "Mom, we can survive for a week without you on duty, and think how glad we'll be when you come home, all refreshed, to take charge again."

Mabel's cautious smile was encouragement enough for Jeanne to begin laying plans.

Jeanne's plan was to arrange a belated honeymoon for her parents, a full week this time, some kind of package deal with lodging and meals already paid for, so those two stay-at-homes couldn't say no at their anniversary supper when she announced the details. Now all she had to do was get her sister and brothers on board, brainstorm about where to make the reservations and how to raise the money, and rope in the grandparents for advice and economic aid.

Danny was too young to imagine that his parents had existed before he was born, but he adored his big sister, so he was eager to go along with Jeanne's scheme. Bruce, at sixteen, was too spooked by girls to contemplate ever going on a honeymoon himself, but he was all in favor of giving his stuck-in-the-mud parents a break from their routines. As the self-appointed romantic of the family, Veronica shared Jeanne's opinion that one night of camping in the Hoosier National Forest was a measly beginning for a marriage. Her view of what constituted a proper honeymoon was derived from reading Victorian novels in which newlyweds took three-month tours of Europe, traveling by private rail car from one resort to another, staying in grand hotels and dancing in ballrooms, or they sailed around the world on an ocean liner, stopping at exotic locations such as Borneo and Tahiti, or they ascended the Nile into the heart of Africa on a paddleboat. Realizing that such lengthy journeys couldn't be crammed into a week, Veronica suggested the parentals might fly to Iceland and visit erupting volcanos. Bruce thought a better idea would be a weeklong stay in a swank hotel in Chicago, with mornings spent in the Museum of Science and Industry, afternoons viewing star shows in the Adler Planetarium, and nights watching Cubs games in Wrigley Field or White Sox games in

Comiskey Park, depending on which team was in town and which park served the tastiest hot dogs. Danny thought Moms and Pops ought to fly on a rocket ship to Mars, look for aliens, take lots of pictures, then fly back home and tell all about their adventures.

Jeanne listened to these ideas patiently and then reminded everyone they were operating on a shoestring budget. The yawning gulf between their budget and their visions became obvious when she began checking prices. Airfares cost an arm and a leg, so that meant the honeymooners would have to travel by road. And given the vintage of their dad's pickup and the family minivan, a five-hour drive might be about the limit, no matter which vehicle they took. This meant Chicago was within range, but she found that the prices of hotels and restaurants there were sky high, as were the prices for tickets to museums and ball games, so she broadened her search to include St. Louis, Cincinnati, Louisville, Columbus, and Indianapolis and found to her dismay that a week's stay in any nearby city would cost far more than the combined savings of all four siblings and more than she could ask the grandparents to chip in from their pensions and social security checks.

Well, if the grandparents couldn't fund the honeymoon, maybe they could think of cheaper options. So Jeanne and her sibs met with the grands in secret, convening in Granny's bedroom over the garage, while the familiar whine of saws and drills sounded from the workshop below. Mamaw Hawkins began by praising the kids for wishing to give their parents a romantic holiday, but perhaps they should scale back their plan from a week to a weekend, which would reduce the cost considerably, and they should also request a veterans' discount, telling the hotel clerk about their father's service in the navy, not on a ship, mind you, but on a bulldozer in the sands of the Middle East, a treacherous place, where he could have been blown up any second, a danger that fortunately he escaped, or else you four darlings wouldn't be here and your father wouldn't be down in the garage making sawdust.

"True enough," Jeanne put in, hoping to pause Mamaw long enough to let the other grands get a word in edgewise.

Papaw Hawkins took advantage of the pause to suggest that the kids should research attractions in less hoity-toity Hoosier cities, like Evansville or Madison or Muncie, and check out budget motels that offer free breakfast, with those make-your-own waffle cookers, and little donuts covered in powdered sugar, and maybe scrambled eggs and grits with biscuits and gravy, and you can snag extra bagels and cream cheese and peanut butter to make sandwiches for lunch and supper, so your food costs go down to zero, and, bingo, you've got an affordable honeymoon weekend.

Granny Mills listened to these musings with an expression on her face that meant she had her thinking cap on, as she liked to say, and when it came her turn to speak, she said mention of the sands of the Middle East reminded her that Gordon had always wanted to visit the Indiana Dunes, ever since he was a boy, but she and her husband had never managed to take him there, since her husband, may he rest in peace, kept raiding their travel kitty to buy booze and got soused pretty much every weekend and often during the week, as on the day when he fell asleep over his lunchtime bottle and was crushed in a stone quarry, which put an end to his wages, as you might imagine, and that was why Gordon quit school and joined the navy and shipped out to the Middle East, where he saw so much wretched desert that he gave up wanting to visit the dunes, imagining they were a sandy wasteland up there on the shore of Lake Michigan, but last week she had showed him an article in *National Geographic* about how there are more kinds of plants and birds and bugs and salamanders in the Indiana Dunes than any other place in the state, and after Gordon had read the story and studied the pictures he said it looked like a paradise.

"It *is* a paradise," said Jeanne, who had studied the ecology of the Indiana Dunes in one of her biology classes. "I'm dying to go there."

"I remember it as a fascinating place," said Mamaw Hawkins. "We took our children there several times when they were growing up, and they loved it, especially Mabel."

"We always stayed in my uncle's rambling old house," said Papaw Hawkins, "just outside the park, within a stone's throw of Lake Michigan."

Jeanne perked up, sensing a possibility. "Does your uncle still live there?"

"He lives in one of those fancy condos for geezers on the north side of Chicago, but his house is still there by the lake. In fact, he's been after me to go up and check on the place, since he doesn't travel anymore, but it's a long drive for me and the missus to take alone, and I'm not the handyman your dad is, so even if I found something out of whack I wouldn't be able to fix it."

"Do you think he'd let Mom and Dad honeymoon there?" Jeanne asked.

"I'm sure he'd be delighted," said Papaw Hawkins. "Especially if your dad offered to take along his toolbox."

"And we could make up a week's worth of meals," Granny Mills suggested, "so all your mother would have to do is warm them up."

"They can walk in the dunes and wade in the lake," said Mamaw Hawkins, "and sleep in any of the five bedrooms."

"They'll have a grand time, and it won't cost them a dime," said Papaw Hawkins.

The kids broke out in cheers, then shushed, remembering their dad down below in the garage, sawing away at some new project.

Except for Mabel and Gordon, who were barred from the kitchen, everyone in the family helped prepare the anniversary supper, including Danny, who stirred the batter for the layer cake and licked the beaters from the icing, licked them so clean, in fact, that he judged they didn't need to be washed. Jeanne overruled him on that point, but otherwise approved his efforts. As the veggie enthusiast, she made a pot of succotash, with corn out of the freezer from last summer's crop and lima beans fresh from the garden. Papaw Hawkins cranked the ice cream maker, now and again adding ice and sprinkles of salt, all the while recounting in fond detail the most scrumptious meals he had ever eaten. The grandmothers bickered about whether the potatoes should be scalloped or mashed, how much celery to include in the stuffing, what oven temperature to use for the persimmon pudding, and numerous other culinary matters, but each time Jeanne stepped in to arbitrate, and no blows were exchanged. When Bruce grumbled on being asked to carve the turkey, Granny Mills told him it would be good practice for carrying out his husbandly duties one day—a prospect that gave Bruce the creeps—for she could say this on behalf of her own late husband, may he rest in peace, whatever his shortcomings, and he had his share, the man was a crackerjack carver of meat.

Meanwhile, as the others chopped and stirred and cooked, Veronica made up place cards for the dining table, writing out each person's name in her fanciest calligraphy and drawing valentine hearts on the cards for her parents. Then she put the final touches on the table centerpiece, which featured a papier-mâché volcano with asters and daisies from the yard poking out of the peak to simulate jets of lava and plastic dinosaurs on loan from Danny scattered around the base to evoke a sense of the married couple's antiquity. Imagine, a quarter century!

Mabel heard a great deal of bustle and laughter from the kitchen and dining room before she was finally invited to the table for the anniversary supper. That flower-bedecked volcano was the first thing she saw, and then she swept her misty gaze over the seven grinning faces of the conspirators who had prepared the meal. The only face missing was Gordon's. He had been dallying in the basement when she came upstairs, saying he needed to trim his beard, of all things, and now everybody was waiting. So she sent Danny to fetch him.

When Danny opened the door to the basement, he noticed at the bottom of the stairs a patch of carpet that looked like the brown-and-yellow fur of a giraffe, one of his all-time favorite animals. "Grub's ready," he called, as Gordon came lumbering into view. "What's with the snazzy rug, Pops?"

Gordon put a finger to his lips. "It's a surprise for Mom."

Danny carried the secret back to the dining room, followed by Gordon, whose beard, Mabel noticed, was as bushy as ever. She motioned for him to sit next to her, instead of in his usual spot at the far end of the table, for Veronica had placed their name cards side by side. Gordon laid his big, callused paw on Mabel's hand, with a touch that seemed to her as tender as on their wedding night, and the two surveyed the feast, the family, the flowers, and volcano, and then everyone joined hands. It happened to be Danny's turn to say grace, an assignment he usually completed with a few quick words in his eagerness to eat, but this evening, inspired by the occasion, he gave thanks for Moms and Pops, who brought him and the sibs into the world, or otherwise he and Brucie and Veronica and Jeanne would still be out there in the place where you live before you're born, and who knows, Granny might be in jail for speeding, only Pops jimmied her car so it couldn't go fast, and Mamaw and Papaw might be sleeping in a haystack somewhere, poor as field mice, says Moms, but instead they're snug as bugs in this old house, and thanks also for animals, especially dinosaurs and giraffes, and thanks for this food and the hands that prepared it, including the hands that stirred the cake batter, and, boy, are we in for a treat, so let's dig in.

Between grace and dessert, Jeanne outlined the honeymoon plan, which brought tears to Mabel's eyes and much blinking to Gordon's, and everybody rhapsodized about the Indiana Dunes, those who had spent time there and those who had only heard or read about that mysterious place. Granny recalled highlights from the *National Geographic* article, Jeanne recited the names of rare plants and butterflies that could be found there, Papaw enthused about the taste of fish cooked over embers on the beach, Bruce speculated about the physics of windblown sand, Veronica predicted that a host of birds would be stopping over there in August on their way south, Mamaw reminisced about moonlit walks along the shore, and Danny proclaimed the dunes must be just about the way coolest place on earth.

As the rhapsody was winding down, Papaw crooked a finger at Danny, who followed him into the kitchen, and soon the two of them returned to the dining room, Papaw carrying the shiny canister from the ice cream maker he had patiently cranked, and Danny carrying the triple-decker cake, which was crowned with twenty-five lit candles. Urged on by much laughter and boisterous advice, Mabel and Gordon made their silent wishes, took in deep breaths, and then blew out the candles with a single puff. Granny served out slices of cake, reserving the largest pieces for her burly son and his bride, and Mamaw added a scoop of strawberry ice cream to each plate. Then all nine mouths were silenced by sweetness.

Early in their marriage, Gordon had insisted that whenever the two of them came to a stairway together, if they were heading up, Mabel should go first, and if they were heading down, he should go first, because that way he would always be one or two steps below her, and so if she tumbled, he could catch her. She humored him, and this became one of the hundreds of habits they formed over the years. And so it happened that Mabel trailed Gordon down the basement stairs after their anniversary feast, and his bulky body kept her from seeing the yellow-and-brown carpet runner at the base of the stairs until she actually stepped on it. Surprised, she exclaimed, "What's this?"

"Your anniversary present," said Gordon, gleeful as always to spring a surprise. "You see the pattern? It looks like a giraffe."

"It certainly does," said Mabel. "Wherever did you find it?"

"In the dumpster behind Flying Carpets and Tile. I checked with the manager, who said there hadn't been much call for it, so I was welcome to take all I wanted."

She ran her gaze along the giraffe pelt from the base of the stairs, past the bathroom door and into the bedroom, where it stopped on her side of the bed. "I appreciate the thought, honey, and the design is certainly striking, but won't it get wet every time there's a hard rain?"

"Nope." Gordon peeled back the edge of the carpet to reveal the planks underneath. "I made a boardwalk, to keep your feet dry, and the rug is to keep them warm."

Mabel tried to say something about the rush of love and gratitude she felt, for this goofy gift, for the feast and the cooks who had prepared it, for the promise of a honeymoon in the dunes, for her crazy, kind husband, for their durable marriage and the lives it had brought into the world, but she couldn't squeeze out any words past the lump in her throat. So she wrapped her arms around him and pressed her face into his chest and bawled.

After all these years of living with Mabel, Gordon still couldn't tell for sure the difference between her sad and happy crying, but since he hadn't done anything boneheaded in the last little while, he guessed this was the happy kind, and so he picked her up and carried her along the boardwalk and laid her gently on the bed. He drew the quilt over her, and she closed her eyes. While she dozed, he took his shower and returned wearing his favorite pair of boxers, the ones decorated with blue horseshoes for the Indianapolis Colts. He slid into his side of the bed, thinking to let her sleep, but she rolled toward him, with a tinkle of copper birds from the necklace she wore, and that was all she wore.

Flood

To consummate their marriage, as polite literature might phrase it, Gordon and Mabel spent their wedding night camping in the Hoosier National Forest, and the next afternoon, mosquito bitten and short on sleep, they drove back to their fixer-upper house in town so they could go to work the following day. To their four children, who came along in due course, a single night in a tent seemed too skimpy an outing to qualify as a honeymoon. So the Mills kids conspired with their grandparents to plan a real honeymoon for Gordon and Mabel, securing the loan of a roomy summer cottage on the shore of Lake Michigan, right next to the Indiana Dunes, where the old married folks could frolic for a week in August, off duty from family and jobs.

Following the silver anniversary supper in June, when the plan was announced, at nearly every family meal the kids gushed about the glories of the dunes and the lake, which they had read and heard about but never seen, and they outdid one another imagining the adventures their parents would have in that fabulous place. Their enthusiasm reached such a pitch, in fact, that Mabel decided she couldn't bear to honeymoon without the children, who after all were the most precious fruit of the marriage. They could also be a pain in the butt or a pang in the heart, she had to admit, but mostly they were precious. And if the kids tagged along, then the grandparents would have to go as well since Papaw Hawkins had a dodgy heart, Mamaw Hawkins had poor balance and arthritic hips, and Granny Mills had a gambling habit and a spacey brain.

Having made up her mind, now Mabel had to persuade Gordon that the whole family should honeymoon together. Even at age fifty, he still had a boyish romantic streak, or maybe it was a goatish streak, so he might have his heart set on a week of marital bliss, just the two of them, as they were on their wedding night, naked under starlight on the shore of Lake Debs in the Hoosier National Forest, stroking one another and swatting mosquitos.

Since Mabel possessed a romantic streak of her own, she had to shake her head to keep from backsliding on her decision, which she planned to wheedle into Gordon's head, hint by hint. She was about to offer the first hint on their after-supper stroll one evening in late July, when Gordon cleared his throat in the way that meant he'd been pondering something.

"Sweetums," he said, "you know I've hankered to see the Indiana Dunes since I was a boy, and my dad was always saying we'd go someday, but what with his drinking and empty wallet we never went, and then he got killed and life hustled me along and now here I am, older than he was when he died, and I haven't taken my own kids to the dunes, so I want them to go with us."

Relieved, Mabel hooked her arm into his and nestled against him. "So do I."

"You do?"

"Absolutely. You can hear how excited the kids are every time they talk about the place, like it's the eighth wonder of the world. So if we go, the kids go." She paused, hesitant about raising the ante, and then added, "The grandparents, too."

Gordon kept silent as they took another few paces along the sidewalk, crickets and katydids filling the evening air with their song. Finally he said, "My mom's never seen the dunes either, bless her heart."

"And my folks love the place, but they haven't been up there since my brothers and I were kids."

"Okay, then, that settles it," said Gordon. "The whole family goes."

It took some arm-twisting to persuade the rest of the family to go, especially Jeanne, who had started the honeymoon conspiracy, and the grandparents, who fretted about being a drag. But eventually all came around, and the Mills household lit up with expectation.

Their expectations were dampened a bit by a thunderstorm that rattled the windows the night before their departure, when rain blew in gusts like joy at a birth or grief at a funeral. Mabel never slept well before a trip, there were so many chores clamoring for attention, and Gordon never could sleep when she was fidgety. So the two of them tossed on their lumpy mattress, dipping into dreams and bobbing up again, as if they were already swimming in Lake Michigan. Even down in their basement bedroom, they could hear the sizzle of rain.

"If the earth could purr, that's how it would sound," said Gordon, quoting his dead father.

"That is the sound of misery heading our way in hip boots," said Mabel, who often felt the need to pull her husband down from the clouds.

Gordon loved rain so much that he forgot it could mean disaster for their trip. So as usual, Mabel worried enough for both of them. She wondered how, with nine people crammed into the van, the suitcases could ride on the roof without getting soaked. What would the kids and grandparents do, cooped up in a cottage beside the lake, if the weather stayed wet? How soggy would the basement get with nobody home to mop it up? Still groggy from sleep and dismayed by the storm, she was about to ask Gordon if he would ever be able to staunch those leaks, but she held her tongue, knowing he prided himself on being able to fix whatever broke at the city garage or in his own house, so the reminder of a fault he couldn't mend was like a sliver under his fingernail.

Instead of fretting about leaks, Gordon welcomed the downpour, for it provided the first real test of the silver anniversary present he had made for Mabel. "You shouldn't need boots to keep your feet dry," he said.

Ah, yes, Mabel remembered, coming fully awake, the boardwalk covered with a carpet runner patterned like the skin of a giraffe, his latest anniversary surprise, meant to spare her from climbing out of bed and stepping into a puddle. There had been puddles on the concrete floor when the two of them first came to look at this house with a realtor, twenty-five years earlier. "The owners scrubbed it down," the realtor explained, "because they wanted everything spanking clean for your visit." Not having grown up around barefaced liars, Gordon and Mabel took the salesman at his word. They had often reminded one another of that lie since buying the house. Over the years, Gordon had painted and patched the limestone walls of the basement from the inside, dug around the foundations and smeared tar on the outside, laid drainage tiles, sprayed sealant on the floor, replaced the downspouts, and installed a sump pump. Yet still, whenever rain hammered down as it was doing tonight, water slid over the concrete like a creek over slate. Somebody at the garage had told Gordon that the bedrock of southern Indiana was old seafloor, and ever since hearing the story he kept imagining that the sea was itching to come back.

"I don't suppose there's any way we could go a different week," Mabel mused into the ticking, trickling darkness.

"This is the only vacation week I've got until next year," said Gordon.

"And we'd never find all of us free again at the same time, anyhow. It's like calling a special session of Congress to schedule a trip with this family."

Gordon could hear Mabel revving herself up to go face the day. The notion of making love crossed his mind, but it crossed slowly, like an old dog, and before he could lift a hand to her breast, Mabel gave a little humph of determination.

"Well," she said, "might as well quit lying here and *do* something." She threw back the covers, sat up, and swung her legs over the side of the bed.

"Enjoy that rug," Gordon said, but Mabel was already padding away toward the bathroom.

A few minutes later, upstairs in the kitchen, she found her ample mother stirring pancake batter and Gordon's wispy mother sitting at the table, purse in lap, hat on head, ready to go, even though it was just past five in the morning. Early rising was not an affliction purely of women, Mabel knew, for her two boys would spring from bed at the least commotion, while the two girls would loll under the covers, even on the morning of a trip, until the last possible second.

"I thought the children should have something solid in their stomachs," said Mamaw Hawkins, lighting a burner on the stove under the griddle.

Mabel grimaced. "I was planning to feed them, Mother."

"Where *are* those slug-a-beds?" Granny Mills asked, in a voice that seemed too big for such a slight woman.

To look at their glad faces, you would never know the sky was cracked wide open and pouring buckets. Mabel kissed the plump cheek of her mother and the papery cheek of Granny Mills, then pushed up her sleeves and set to work.

Out in the garage, where he had shoved aside bicycles and boxes and bundled newspapers the night before to make room for the van, Gordon checked the spare tire, the battery, the oil, all the while tingling from the sound of rain on the roof. He made sure the jumper cables and road tools were on board, along with his bucket of home fix-it tools that he might need at the house where they would be staying. The long-suffering Dodge—which was older than the combined ages of Danny and Veronica—hardly ever gave him trouble, since he looked after it himself, but the tools came in handy for helping stranded drivers of less reliable cars.

Gordon's father had rarely passed a stalled car on the road without stopping to help. The old man was not much use when drunk, but he was a wizard with machines when sober. Drunk or sober, he loved rain, the harder the better, with lightning and thunder and thrashing trees and greenhouse air. When Gordon was a young squirt and a storm roared through, his father used to wrap him in a blanket and carry him outside onto the porch to listen and watch. All these years later, lightning still made the air smell of whiskey for Gordon and sent a scurry of pleasure along his spine. Even aboard ship in the navy, when a gale blew rain and waves across the deck, and every other sailor had taken shelter, he would stand gripping the rail, eyes shut, and imagine himself back on that porch, wrapped in the arms of his father.

What Gordon needed right now was something waterproof to wrap around the suitcases. All his tarps were spread over heaps of salvaged lumber and rusty machine parts in the backyard. He stood for a moment in the doorway of the garage, deciding which pile to uncover, then he took off his shoes and socks, rolled up his jeans, and splashed out into the rain to grab one of the blue tarps. He laid this over the roof rack on the van, wet side down, and later, when the sleepy boys bumbled out from the kitchen lugging suitcases, the smell of pancakes wafting out with them, Gordon loaded everything into the tarp, folded over the corners as neatly as any package, and tied everything down with rope.

After breakfast, which even the girls straggled down for—Veronica frizzy and daubed in the fashion of her middle school, Jeanne looking thrown together in the manner of a coed late for class—Gordon loaded the coolers and jugs and bags into the van, then everybody climbed in. The shocks groaned. Danny pushed the button on the garage door opener, and they drove into a waterfall.

From her navigator's spot in the front, Mabel swung around and called, "Don't forget to close the door!" But Danny, who was devoted to pushing buttons, had already pushed this one again, and Gordon could see in the rearview mirror that the garage was clamped shut. Before they cleared the Limestone city limits, Mabel had asked each grandparent and child at least one question—about locking windows and turning off hair curlers and packing underwear. She had to shout to make herself heard above the roar of rain, especially when questioning her father, who was nearly deaf even when he wore what he called those blasted hearing aids. "Papaw," she yelled, "do you have your blood pressure pills?"

Papaw Hawkins, in the middle seat, cupped a hand to his ear and leaned forward. Mamaw Hawkins answered for him: "Yes, dear. We've thought of everything."

"Gracious," said Granny Mills, who was perched on the edge of the front seat, leaning toward the windshield, "you can't see whether you're coming or going."

"I can see fine, Mom," Gordon said, although in fact the wipers failed to keep up with the rain, and so as they rolled beyond the final streetlamps, the road appeared as a gray blur, and his cataracts turned the headlights of oncoming traffic into hazy stars.

"We won't have a dry stitch to put on when we get there," Mabel muttered. "If we get there."

"Who tied up that tarp, I ask you, and who's driving this fine vehicle?" said Gordon. He reached down to pat Mabel reassuringly on the thigh, and instead smacked the road atlas, which she had opened across her lap.

"No shortcuts on this trip," she said, believing in highways as fervently as Gordon believed in back roads.

"I keep telling you, we were never lost," he answered.

"Then why did we spend half a day zigzagging through the boon-docks?"

"I wanted the kids to see Indiana's lesser-known attractions."

"Don't squabble, dears," Granny Mills urged.

From the back, Danny started singing, "Oh, what a beautiful morn-ing!" and Bruce joined in, then Veronica and Jeanne, then one by one the grandparents, then Gordon and finally Mabel, their voices quavery as though they were singing underwater, as in a sense they were.

The family kept singing for more than an hour. Whenever they finished one song, somebody remembered another one, verse after verse, but gradually their voices petered out. By the time they left the Indianapo-lis ring road, with its comforting islands of light, and headed north on the interstate over dark plains of soybeans and corn, past regiments of wind turbines, they had fallen silent.

Mile after mile, they drove on through the downpour. Now and again a truck or car would pass them, throwing up oily spray, and the red taillights would dwindle away, or oncoming headlights would shine blearily for a moment and then vanish, but otherwise there was nothing to see except the white edge lines and center reflectors leaping at them from the gloom. Everyone in the van felt some degree of fear, from the mild unease of Danny, who kept watch through the window for the fins of sharks, to the steady alarm of Mabel, who imagined power lines blown down across the road and bridges washed out. Even Gordon, rarely one to fret, wished he had gone ahead and bought that new set of tires when Firestone had them on sale because the old treads were feeling snaky on the slick pavement.

The burbling sounds and watery murk put Gordon in mind of the submarine movies he used to watch as a kid with his dad—the crew breathing inside a capsule of air surrounded by ocean, the captain barking "Dive, dive!" when the enemy was detected, the sailors listening to the beep of sonar as a destroyer chugged by overhead, their faces tense with waiting for the concussion of depth charges.

"How much farther, Daddy?" Veronica called.

"Another hundred miles, kiddo," Gordon answered.

Bruce yelled, "What's to eat?"

"You just ate," said Mabel.

Presently the gloom up ahead was broken by the flashing of hazard lights, from a car pulled onto the shoulder. Mabel could sense when Gordon took his foot off the accelerator, and she said firmly, "Oh, no you don't."

"I just want to see what's the matter."

"You'll get us all sideswiped by a semi."

"Think if it was you there in a broken-down car," said Gordon, tapping the brake and coasting to a stop behind the flashers, "or Papaw or one of the kids."

"You know very well Papaw doesn't drive any more, dear," Mamaw Hawkins put in.

"It could be gangsters," Granny Mills observed. "We're not all that far from Chicago."

Danny and Veronica were echoing "Gangsters? Gangsters!" and Mabel was repeating Gordon's name through clenched teeth as he climbed out of the van.

He opened an umbrella, which gave scant protection from the slanting rain, then sloshed to the driver's door of the stranded car. The window slid down an inch, and the pimply, frightened face of a teenage boy peered up at him. Gordon asked, "Got a problem, buddy?"

The boy said nothing, going pale, shaking. He clung with both hands to the steering wheel.

Even after all these years, Gordon could not get used to scaring people. Squat, husky, dark—like a heavy-browed lab assistant or dungeon

guard from a horror movie, as the kids had remarked over the years—
he stood there in the deluge trying to look harmless. Rain swirling
around the umbrella had already soaked him from the knees down. He
forced a grin and repeated his question: "You got a problem?"

This time the boy answered in a pinched voice: "I was just driving
along, and it like conked out, and now it won't start."

"Gas okay?" Gordon asked.

"Half a tank."

"Did you run through some water?"

"The whole road's full of water."

"Any deep stuff, I mean," Gordon said.

The boy shrugged. "Could be. I don't remember."

As she watched all this, Mabel kept thinking, Lord, let him not be
some nut with a gun. Granny Mills was reciting the exploits of famous
Chicago gangsters. Mamaw and Papaw Hawkins agreed that drug runners might choose a foul day like this one to sneak along the highways.
The children kept scouring the steamed-up windows for a better view.

Gordon leaned away from the car, a vintage Mustang, and reckoned
he knew what was wrong. "Pop that hood, will you? I'll be right back."

Figuring the boy would be too spooked to get out of the car and help,
Gordon walked back to the van and fetched Bruce, along with a rag, a
roll of duct tape, a screwdriver, and a flashlight from the toolbox.

Since waking to thunder that morning, Bruce had been itching for
an excuse to get out in the rain, so he accompanied his father without
a grumble. Now he stood holding the umbrella in one hand, flashlight
in the other, while Gordon bent under the hood of this stranger's car.
"Wet plugs?" Bruce guessed.

"Points," said Gordon. He showed Bruce the crack in the distributor
cap, showed how to seal it with duct tape, how to dry the rotor arm and
contact points, turning the rag and wiping carefully, then how to put
everything back together with the spring clips, just as Gordon himself
had been shown by his own father. Satisfied, Gordon peered around

the hood, twirled an index finger in the air, and hollered at the driver, "Try it!"

The engine cranked a few times, coughed, caught, and finally roared. Gordon slammed the hood. He and Bruce paused beside the car long enough for the driver to mumble thanks and for Gordon to advise him to change that distributor cap first thing. "You go on," he added, "and we'll follow you a ways to make sure it's running okay."

But the Mustang disappeared into the storm well before Gordon and Bruce could slide onto the blankets that had been spread over their seats, before Gordon could get the van up to cruising speed, before Bruce could squelch the talk of gangsters and drug runners, and even then, for mile after slick mile, fear kept a grip on all their throats.

The children soon relaxed enough to play euchre, their laughter punctuated by the slap of cards. Papaw Hawkins resumed his commentary on the crops, livestock, barns, and farm implements that loomed up through the torrential rain. Lulled by the steady rumble, the two grandmothers dozed off. When Mabel joined them, nodding against the head rest, hands twitching with sleep on the map book in her lap, Gordon was able to pull off the interstate and follow a back road that he calculated would cut seven miles off the trip. Immediately he felt a surge of excitement.

"Hogs," Papaw Hawkins was saying. "Poland Chinas, looks like, although could be Berkshires, with that mushed-up snout."

The land stretched away flat and muddy to the horizon, a barely visible line interrupted only by silos and woodlots. The ditches on both sides of the road were full to the brim, the creeks were spilling over their banks, and in all that level countryside there seemed no place for the water to go, while rain kept sluicing down.

Gordon could tell they were nearing the dunes when the land began to roll. Each rise they came to was a bit higher, each trough deeper. The pavement on this two-lane road crumbled into gravel and weeds at the shoulder, so he kept the Dodge hugging the center stripe, except when he had to make way for the few oncoming vehicles, mainly pickups. A couple of drivers waved at him through bleary windshields, their hands jerking like white flags, but whether in greeting or warning he couldn't be sure. The uncertainty made him ease up on the gas.

Even so, as they topped another rise and went skimming down, there was no way he could have braked in time to keep from plowing into the pooled water at the bottom of the hill. The van shuddered from the impact, silencing Papaw Hawkins, halting the kids' laughter and the slap of cards, waking Mabel and the grandmothers. In the second it took Mabel to grab his knee and cry "What is it?" Gordon had lost control and was merely tapping the useless brakes, gripping the useless wheel, listening to the engine sputter and stall. The Dodge wallowed to a stop in water that reached halfway to the windows.

Amid the shrieks and murmurs, Danny's high-pitched voice rang clear: "Wow! It's a flood!"

Those words hushed everyone, even Danny. For a few moments, the only sound was the drumming of rain on the roof.

Gordon sat there trying to decide if this was the dumbest thing he had ever done, when Granny Mills jerked her tiny feet from the floormat and wailed, "Lordy, it's coming in."

Sure enough, water was leaking from the engine compartment and around the doors.

"Gordon," Mabel said in a strained voice, "this is a shortcut, right?"

"It's a scenic route."

"And the car's not going to start, is it?"

"Not any time soon." He thought forlornly of his tools packed under the seat, the gleaming wrenches and pliers, which would be of no use for reviving a drowned engine.

"Oh, my! We're stranded!" Mamaw Hawkins exclaimed.

"What are we going to *do*, Daddy?" Veronica cried.

We could die, Gordon thought, we really could, if we don't get out of here and the flood keeps rising. A family, a car, a hog, a stone: it was all the same to water. But it was not all the same to him, for he loved each person here with a bright and energizing love. So he straightened up and said, "We're going wading, that's what."

"I don't think—" Mabel began.

"We're going wading," he repeated. Mabel gave him a look, and then tightened her lips. "Now Danny and Veronica," Gordon went on, "you scoot up here to the front and be careful you don't trample Granny."

He cranked down his window, wriggled out through the opening, cursing his bulk and the hitch in his back, then he stood on the road in water waist-deep. The two children clambered over Mamaw and Papaw and into the driver's seat, Danny first, then Veronica. As they stretched their arms out to Gordon, he pulled them through the window and set them cross-legged on the hood. "Don't go away," he said.

Rain hammered on his skull, on the tarp, on the gleaming curved steel of the van. He stuck his dripping face back inside.

Before he could speak, Granny Mills inquired, "Should we take off our shoes?"

"No, Mom, don't take off your shoes."

"But they'll ruin."

Mabel put an arm across her mother-in-law's bony shoulders, allowing Gordon to say, "Okay, troops. I'm going round to open the doors, and when I do, there'll be a rush of water. Sit tight while it levels out. It will rise to just above the level of the seats. Imagine you're splashing in Lake Michigan. Then I want you to come out slowly, one by one."

Nobody panicked, but their elbows and knees were twitchy as Gordon helped them out, his mother first, because she was so frail, then the others, until they all stood huddled together in brown froth beside the car.

Jeanne shivered. "It's cold!"

"It's filthy," said Mamaw Hawkins.

"Topsoil and manure," Papaw Hawkins observed. "Nothing wrong with that, although the farmers are going to wish they had it back on their fields."

Now where? Gordon wondered. They couldn't stay in this swale between ridges, with the water inching higher. But which direction should they take? They had not passed a light for several miles before the van foundered, so the nearest farmhouse back south would be miles away, too far for the old folks to wade, and a stretch even for the younger kids. To the east and west, the fields were flooded, only the tips of fenceposts showing. He decided the safest path lay to the north, toward the dunes and the lake. The family needed to stay close together and keep moving until they reached higher ground.

As he explained to the others what they had to do, they could hear the steel in his voice, and no one balked, not even his mother, when he lifted her onto his back. The legs clasping his waist and the arms clasping his neck felt brittle. Bruce backed against the hood of the van so Danny could climb onto his shoulders, then the two of them set off, Bruce placing his feet carefully so as not to slip, Danny peering ahead as he imagined a sailor might do from the crow's nest on a ship. Jeanne and Veronica hooked their arms together and followed the boys. Mamaw and Papaw Hawkins held hands, then Mabel took her mother by the elbow and Gordon braced her father. All touching, bumping into one another, they slogged uphill, dragging their feet along the drowned pavement.

Partway up the slope, Gordon staggered on loose gravel, lurched, and then steadied himself. His mother cried "Whoops!" and her thin forearm tightened against his throat. As the rain kept pelting down, he caught a whiff of whiskey, so sharp that it might have laced the actual air and not merely his memory, and he thought of his father, gone under, gone under.

Suddenly, from his perch atop Bruce's shoulders, Danny sang out, "Hey, Pops! It's the northern lights!"

"Not likely, son. Not in this rain."

"Really, Pops," Danny insisted, pointing ahead. "I can see over the next hill, and it's shining up there."

In that moment, all four of the children felt a shiver of pleasure as they remembered sitting beside their father in the pickup, high on the mountain of trash, watching curtains of light dance on the horizon. Gordon felt the same shiver of delight, as if in that instant he and his children shared one mind, one heart.

After a few more steps up the slope, the spell was broken, as they all could see the source of the shining—a pair of blazing headlights, framed between two rows of amber running lights, one down low across the bumper and one up high across the top of the cab, and strings of red lights outlining the trailer.

"It's only a semi," Danny said, his voice sagging from disappointment. Then, realizing that a truck could mean rescue, he cried, "Hey, it's a semi!"

It was a semi, alright, stopped maybe a hundred yards ahead. Did the driver see them? Gordon wondered. Needing both arms to support his mother, he couldn't wave, but he didn't need to, as the headlights flashed three times, the horn blared once, and the truck rolled slowly toward the family, who had gathered in a clump around Gordon.

"Cast your bread upon the waters," his mother whispered into his ear.

"What's that, Mom?"

"Cast your bread upon the waters, for you will find it after many days."

"There's plenty of water," Gordon said to humor her, "but where's the bread?"

"Right there," she said, pointing to the truck as it came to a stop beside their wet little troop. "That's your bread come back to you. To us."

Puzzling out what she meant would have to wait for a calmer time. Right now, the driver was waving for them to climb in, and all nine squeezed into the cab and sleeper compartment, dripping water.

"Where you headed?" asked the driver, a sixtyish man with a bald scalp and grizzled beard.

"North," said Gordon. "Toward the dunes."

"So am I, heading back to Gary, just as soon as I can turn this rig around."

"We're ever so thankful," said Mabel.

"No need for thanks, ma'am. I've been helped plenty myself."

The kids piled into the sleeper loft, where they swapped bigger and bigger stories about the terrible flood, with laughter and relief in their voices. Mamaw and Papaw Hawkins sat up front next to the driver and began asking him questions, for it wasn't every day they got to talk with a Black man, and they meant to make the most of the opportunity. On the bench seat behind them, Granny Mills nestled against Gordon from one side, Mabel from the other, each trying to warm up against his tired body. Mabel wrapped an arm around his waist and pressed her cheek against his chest. "I've never felt your heart thumping so hard," she said.

"That's because I've never done such a boneheaded thing before."

"Hush, now. We're safe. We're together. Nothing else matters."

Gordon started to say he felt ashamed for endangering his family, but Mabel pressed a finger against his lips and said again, "Hush," and he did hush, and let go of his worry for the moment, let go of his sorrow, listening to the music of his children laughing, Mamaw and Papaw chatting with the driver, his mother lightly snoring, Mabel sighing, and surrounding them all, embracing them all, the innocent speech of the rain.

SCOTT RUSSELL SANDERS is the author of more than twenty books of fiction, essays, and personal narrative, including *Hunting for Hope*, *A Conservationist Manifesto*, *Dancing in Dreamtime*, and *Earth Works: Selected Essays*. His most recent book is *The Way of Imagination*, a reflection on healing and renewal in a time of social and environmental upheaval. Based in Bloomington, Indiana, he is Distinguished Professor Emeritus of English at Indiana University and a fellow of the American Academy of Arts and Sciences.